T0208690

WORLD IS WOMAN

WORLD IS WOMAN

by Terry Midkiff

iUniverse books may be ordered through booksellers or by contacting:

iUniverse
1663 Liberty Drive
Bloomington, IN 47403
www.iuniverse.com
1-800-Authors (1-800-288-4677)

Because of the dynamic nature of the Internet, any web addresses or links contained in
this book may have changed since publication and may no longer be valid. The views
expressed in this work are solely those of the author and do not necessarily reflect the
views of the publisher, and the publisher hereby disclaims any responsibility for them.

ISBN: 978-1-4401-8748-3 (sc)
ISBN: 978-1-4401-8746-9 (hc)
ISBN: 978-1-4401-8747-6 (e)

Cover design, Terry Midkiff

Library of Congress Control Number: 2009911564

Print information available on the last page.

iUniverse rev. date: 02/15/2016

O, strange passing world—

PART I

▼

I

▼

FRIDAY. 6:47 PM.

You can live in Austin for centuries. It's always there. A free-for-all.
An oasis of hippies, slackers, bead sellers, alcoholics, pimps, druggies,
vegetarians, gurus, professors, punks, bums, posers, Jezebels, jewels,
sophisticates, suburbanites, tech heads, Republicans, Democrats,
Independents, capitalists, California transplants, land developers,
business schemers, Asians, Africans, a few Europeans, a few Arabs, a
few Hindus, various drifters, music makers, socialists. Various thieves,
good-for-nothings, shitheads, preachers, screamers gathered in the
campus square. Everybody loves it. Nobody ever leaves. Or if they do,
they always come back.

It's sticky here. Fertile. Sometimes you're just dying to leave, but
you can't. It's a habit. A cigarette. A lover. You sit and look around, do
nothing, go see a movie at The Dobie, smile, sit on the porch. Feeling
justified, international, lazy. It's disgusting.

Actually, everything has caved in on me. Everything and nothing.
An onslaught of circumstance. Miniature and huge and always fresh.
But I am delighted. I eat ash, bits of wood, Sheetrock, diamonds, roots,
microchips. Yes, yes … a true paradise.

Buildings have fallen. Trees have burned. Bodies have lain. Still, the absurd curiosity. I show my teeth. I growl. I bite. I laugh. I make something from nothing.

And more and more lately, Morton and I have been finding ourselves at The Crazy Lady. A cheap cabaret. Yes. A classy dive, to be sure. And the young foxes aren't half bad. A bit wacky, a little strung out and fussy, a little jealous, tattooed here and there, but all in all very adapted and congenial. In short, a fine group! Not nearly as green-eyed as you might expect. Conversation is a menu item. They know I haven't much money. I give it all to them. But it seems honesty merits special treatment. It is a tonic, an ointment for loneliness, even if only temporary, this gazing at all the lovelies. A supreme pastime, indulged in every so often. Something not unrelated to a dog chasing his tail. Around we go. Around and around.

We enter thrice weekly, laughing, in good spirits. Within minutes a couple of temptresses have plopped themselves down on our contented laps, and we are sipping drinks and exchanging pleasantries. It is all absurd, of course, but the smell of food is sometimes better than the meal itself. The imagination grills it to perfection.

We sit around, everything and everyone in a flattering light. We ask how business is that evening, laugh, banter back and forth, fend off accusations of being regulars. My eyes quite naturally slip down to a garter belt while they are talking. Such succulent thighs and hips. Absolute magic. Amazing! The miracle of the ages! Smoothness beyond comprehension! And such luscious bulging breasts. Kept warm and cozy and happy inside two half-nests of white lace.

It's a dream. You go in there for the dream. The dream of beautiful women. All the hair, all the breasts, all the little dresses and lingerie and legs and high heels, all the little outfits and stockings and faces. The marvelous explosion and sight of so much beauty, so many fleshy warm curves, so many arched backs, so many flared rumps, so many scantily clad sumptuous young women. Unbelievable!

It's all an illusion—but this is beside the point. You go in there to work the illusion, to soak up the beauty and to learn from it. To learn how these little creatures operate. How the world operates. It is the same to some extent even on the outside. But this isn't the outside. This is the inside. The inside where, for twenty dollars or less, an exquisite young woman will squirm in front of you all but naked. And she will look at you, and keep on looking at you, and bathe you in her glow. It's like water to a thirsty, dry mouth. You forget about everything. You forget that you are sitting in a club just off the lower level of the interstate. You forget that there are people sitting around you. You forget even about the music. You forget, forget, forget. You're too busy playing and frolicking and imagining and drinking in, say … the arch of her back and the warm fleshy firmness of her legs … and the heart-shaped trick of nature that is her ass.

Sometimes you go in there on off nights and it's simply a bunch of vultures strutting around on two legs in mini dresses. Going from table to table. Anything that looks like money, and they'll swoop down on you … bending down with their breasts threatening to burst out of the fabric at any moment. They'll place these right in your face and say, "Do you want a dance?" or "Would you like some company?" Especially if you're an old fart or a businessman or seem to have money to burn.

Usually I dismiss these offers with a polite "No, but thank you very much" and a small wink. And if they aren't too much of a little witch, they will smile and flap off somewhere else. They know how it works.

But if they are exceptionally gorgeous, or even if they are rather plain and just seem to be having a rough night, I sometimes allow them to sit down, assuming that none of my favorites is there.

If one of my favorites is there—for example, Jeanine or … or Rachel, then my money naturally goes to them.

Yes. And a little later on tonight I must call on Morton. Yes. He's getting desperate, it seems, to find some little wench there he can spend the evenings with. It's on his mind constantly. He gets worked up about it. Every now and then he gets disgusted. Sitting there at Les Amis Cafe, stroking his attempt at a beard.

Tonight, tonight … yes, I think it's his birthday or something. I'll have a few little birds lined up for him at The Lady. Yes. We'll have drinks and everything. It's where we spend our money. Supporting their habits, most likely. We'll sit around … the girls will be talking nonsense of course. My little muse … Jeanine is her name. She's dancing for him. I don't mind. She doesn't mind. He surely doesn't mind! Nobody minds! She'll shake it for him … winking at me. I'll laugh, tap my cigarette … look over at him, make sure he's enjoying it …

The damn phone is ringing. I reach over there.

"Crazy Lady Cabaret … "

"Hello, may I speak to Gerald, please?"

"Oh, Aaron—I thought you were Morton." (Besides Morton, there is only Aaron and Jens that matter these days. Everyone else has died. Oh, and Kian.)

He doesn't want to join us. I don't blame him. Aaron is a spiritualist. A guru. He wants Nirvana … goddamn it! And he's going to get it! He knows what the hell's going on! Yes. He has Herculean powers of faith and devotion. But he can't get rid of his big flapping Eastern blinders. He's lost in a forest of mysticism. He masturbates at the very thought of India.

But I fancy him. If I had a harem I would give him two of my wives to be at his disposal. But he wouldn't have this.

Aaron probably needs The Lady more than any of us. Well, maybe not more than Morton. Might as well be serious for a minute.

Yes. It's a temporary addiction, and thus I keep going. I'm getting to know all the hotties. All their little quirks and mannerisms and movements onstage and favorite drinks and so forth. Top Shelf Margarita, no salt … Cuervo Gold, extra salt … rum and Coke, easy on the Coke, etc. I'm even starting to picture different minds in different bodies. Edie's mind in Gina's body. Edie's mind in Rachel's body. Rachel's body in Edie's mind. Joan's mind AND body in, over, and around everything. Wait, no … my mind on Edie's body. Edie's body on my bed. Wait … no, no … SHERRY'S BODY, in Rachel's dream, on my mind, with Jeanine's whip … IN GINA'S BED! But with Heidi's legs.

Yes. I am currently living at 716C Harris Avenue. Off Duval and 34th Street. A large brown room in the trees atop a little yellow house. Not yellow like piss, but yellow like flowers that have been sitting in the windowsill for two or three days. The water murky, needing to be changed.

Everything is basically shitty, but I laugh and wallow around in my freedom. I look around, snicker at my sudden absence from my job, scratch my chin. I am a little troll. I think of the next millennia and yawn.

2

▼

SATURDAY. 12:14 PM.

I wake up, peer out the blinds, look back in at the room. It's about noon. The sun is shining down in here. Sometimes it's so gaudy and offensive. I have my bed situated up beside a little trio of windows so I can watch any goings-on out in the street or the yard. I'll probably lie here all afternoon. What could be better? Of course I'll have to get some food at some point in the day. That'll mean leaving my tree briefly.

I adjust my blanket, get situated. I will try to remember last night. Morton. Yes. He lost all control. Spent all my money ... and his, too. The little strumpet ... Jeanine. We've been going to breakfast after she gets off at the club. I am in love with her. But I can't decide between her and Rachel.

I remember the first night we went out with her. Jeanine. She had just finished dancing for me. We were sitting around a table. Her, Morton, and I. She was putting her top back on and adjusting it around her breasts and complaining about needing a ride home. Yes. And who was there to give it to her but myself? I casually brought up the possibility. We felt each other out. I tried to reassure her. We giggled. She tossed it over, sat down, lit a cigarette. We made conversation. I tried to put her at ease. It helped that she had seen me in there many times before. I couldn't help it. She is such a delightful young dish. With her pointed, mischievous little face. With her high cheekbones and long black hair. And always dressed in pleated little skirts and long white stockings.

Finally, she agreed to a late-night snack and so, eventually, we made it out of the club and decided to walk down to a little restaurant for some dessert and conversation. Yes. Walking down the sidewalk with this little thing beside you finally and it's two o'clock in the AM and Morton there too and her asking you where you're from again and where you live and so forth.

Soon we turned in to a café and were seated in a little booth as Morton staggered off to find a restroom. We lit cigarettes, got comfortable. She perked up, exhaled.

"Ya'll are odd. But I like you. I'm glad you're not weird or anything. I didn't think you were."

She was sitting there. Beaming. Looking quite friendly and lovely.

"I've noticed that you've been coming in a lot lately."

"Oh."

She started laughing.

"No, I like it. It's nice. Actually, you're pretty much my favorite customers now."

A few seconds passed. She played with her cigarette in the ashtray.

"You know what?"

"What?"

"You're funny. Your expressions. I like dancing for you. You're easy to dance for."

It was slightly exhilarating being there with her. And rather refreshing. This young little thing sitting across from you who danced in a club for money. This little trick of youth and beauty chattering away.

We stayed there for maybe a half-hour or so. Her chattering away about this, that, and the other. About where she moved from, what she wanted to do in life, how she couldn't handle certain jobs, etc.

Since then we've made an odd sort of acquaintance. It's touched with intoxicants. With dollars and circumstance. It will end sometime most likely as it began.

But when you are there with her back in the club and she is flashing her little smile and tilting her head back and squirming around on you with her back arched and her dark hair cascading gently down her shoulders ... when she is like this you think something entirely different. Then she is no longer the girl you go out to breakfast with. She's more like some queen vixen of your imagination ... completely manifested and true to life. Yes. Truer than life!

Oh yes, but back to last night. What I recall of it, that is. Which isn't much. I remember Morton lost all control. We didn't have a dime left on us by the time we left. Luckily for him it was his birthday, and he got to sit back for free while Jeanine and Edie rubbed their asses all over him all night. Meanwhile, I had to fork out a twenty every time.

And I kept having to shoo off all the other flocks of breasts that were always trying to congregate around our table whenever Jeanine and Edie were called away to the main stage. When all the other skirts see a lot of dancing going on at the tables, it draws them over like flies. They're all over trying to sniff out some money. It's like a little wildlife preserve during a feeding. All these ravens and vultures and hawks and these flapping birds of prey that had been circling up above for hours all coming in and landing and squawking and fighting. They come flying in from all corners. And a few others come running over on the ground. All trying to pick at what's left of my wallet every time Jeanine and Edie would get up for the least little thing. This big commotion and cacophony of beaks and tits and feathers and legs, flapping and pecking and screeching all around us.

A veritable zoo of asses and bosoms, all in their natural habitat. A Serengeti! Right down the highway! All night long!

3

▼

MONDAY. 12:57 PM.

Last night I was at Jeanine's. Yes. She's been letting me come over and get high with her.

She was sitting there in her slip ... up on the bed ... curled around with her legs underneath her and leaning back up against the pillows ... smoking cigarettes and dabbing the end of a joint around in the ashtray.

It was late in the evening.

Suddenly, she pipes up.

"Do you like my cat?"

I look down at the cat. His eyes blink absentmindedly as he looks off. A small white Persian ... idiotic beast ... getting his head scratched up on the bed with this little doe. He seemed to be contemplating something. Maybe his litter box ... or entropy ... or his water bowl or something.

"Oh it's nice. It's very pretty."

I was sitting in a chair beside her bed. I lit a cigarette, looked up at her face. I pictured her at the club. She caught this. She gave a little smile, trailed off with some little stream of leftover thought, looked off.

"You know … when I'm up on stage … I'm completely off in my own little world. I'm almost oblivious to everyone watching. It's like my own little game. My own little show. It doesn't even feel like it's me up there. It's like somebody else, and I'm being them for a while … "

I smiled. All this from Port Arthur, Texas. And so young. Barely even twenty. But she had the instinct.

"I'm glad you like me. I remember one time … one of the first times I saw you in there … you didn't tip me. You walked off or something, or you didn't seem interested in me. It sort of pricked my ego … to have a young guy … not notice me and not watch me … I enjoy dancing for you … you don't slobber all over me like some guys do … and you make eye contact. And you don't pressure me about anything … "

I looked around her room. Lots of white and lace and shoes and mirrors and clothes and slips strung up everywhere. I sat there for about an hour as she chirped away about this, that, and the other.

Eventually I got up to leave, but for a while I sat there. Listening to her. Talking on and on. This little thing. With so many hidden abilities. So many diverse talents. You'd never have guessed it. Such a small face. In such the big city!

Yes. She's the latest in an annual spring hatching of little butterflies that continually decorate the earth. All the life and the centuries, all the images … the endless succession of moments … the bullshit … the spinning, chaotic, ant farm of it all, and yet the world still comes out with a little Jeanine every year. Strange and cheerful and obliging. Stepping onto the stage and gliding up to the pole. Twirling around and taking it all off.

4

▼

WEDNESDAY. 4:51 PM.

All last week I've been sitting at Star Seeds. A splendid little diner. Dirty. Stylish. East side. Just down from The Lady. I go in around midnight, order turkey on a kaiser roll with bacon and coffee.

Yes. The late-night crowd. An interesting array of specimens. Youth, women in black, various goths, strippers, slackers, down-and-outers, musicians, film freaks, the occasional tie-and-button-down, charlatans, drinkers, hangers-on.

I usually go in high, red-eyed. Sometimes it's sensory overload, and I just sit there. Smoke. Take in any lovelies that may be perched around and jabbering.

Oh, but last night. Yes. Nowhere to be. Nestled down in my booth. Everything twinkling and clinking. Everything interesting and worthy of note or a second glance. Watching the kitchen. This strange bear of a man with a large white outfit on. Flesh everywhere. Scraggly hair. I catch glimpses of him ambling around back there. Turning the order wheel, adjusting his music, moving around in his little domain of food. And the waitress. A young pleasant girl of about twenty-four. Long brown hair. Thin face. Slightly attractive. She wheels in behind the counter and glides quickly up to the plates and all in one motion she turns around, plates in hand, and is suddenly back around from the counter, striding down the aisle. Down she comes. Down between the stools and the booths. Her face is one of purpose ... with little mental tasks going on behind it. And then she drops off the plates and turns back behind the counter again for the coffee that she promptly delivers to my table, where she refills my cup with a playful smile.

I watch her walk off, take the creamer, pour it into my cup. I stir the sugar in gently. Then a nice large swallow and a pull from my cigarette.

I sit there. Buzzed. Everything seems to flow. The edges are soft. I look around ... content ... impish. Sitting there in my booth. Occasionally the moment builds, and I feel myself on the verge of a small outburst. I jerk my head to the side ... look off oddly ... staring at some spot maybe on the wall.

Soon my food arrives. Immediately all this energy and matter and sustenance sitting in front of your eyes, and I give a little giggle as I proceed to devour my sandwich ravenously. It is unbelievably good. All this delicious texture and flavor and warmth going down the gullet and into the stomach. And you make love to a bite ... all the turkey and the bacon and the bread rolling around in your mouth, and you are salivating and happy and pacified and giddy.

I swallow, caress my mouth for a second with my tongue, pick up my coffee, drink deep and heartily ... pause. And then the next bite. And the next.

I think of Rachel and Jeanine, all the cooing little doves over at The Lady ... chirping away, strutting around the tables, some sitting down to nest. The whole place full of them. Squawking in the dressing room, singing on the stage, fluttering and hovering around the bar. I think of all the sex, the beauty, the need, the affirmation, all the money, all the food all around me being prepared and eaten. I think of all the strength, all the strange exotic shapes of flesh and matter and molecules feeding the art of it all ... playing the beautiful, off-key, ridiculous melody of it all. I think of all this, and it strikes me again that I have nowhere to go. That I am already there.

It is the same everywhere. The design of things. I relate to it simply. Bodily.

It happens when you're sitting around one day by yourself. Staring at a spot on your sleeve maybe. Fingering a little piece of thread. It is in the suddenness of something grasped, in the smallest of small things, that you sense, on some special evening, in some special moment, a decidedly faded gesture of acknowledgment. A sense of relief. Of release somehow. From everything.

There is a lightness. A sort of birth. A willful, robust birth, born from disappointment. Disappointment in what used to be called Success or Happiness. Or Eternity. Or Purpose. Or Truth. All of these are insufficient concepts. They have no meaning anymore for me. They fall on deaf ears. They had their chance. And they squandered it.

Now I have Purpose. My own Purpose. I am Purpose.

And still the days come. I see them to the door and make room for more. Here they are. Here they are and here we go.

5

▼

SUNDAY. 2:41 PM.

Last night, a new one. The Lady again. Yes.

I walk in, find a table, sit down and light a cigarette. The waitress comes quickly over in her short, tight little skirt to take my drink order. Whiskey ... sour.

Suddenly your drink arrives, and you put down your cigarettes and fold out your little green bills, and then the drink is at your lips and it is chilled and alcoholic ... a zesty, stiff, bright, oak color easing down your throat.

The bold, magic reality of the forms hits you again. I tip freely. As usual. Tipping consists of getting up from your table and walking up to the edge of the main stage at the center of the club and having the dancer slink or crawl over to you in the middle of her session and wriggle just for you for a few seconds, at which point you slip her a couple dollars that she tosses to the center of the stage in her little pile. Yes. But soon I am spotted and another form is back at my table waiting on me. I join her, allow her to stay seated.

Some of them seem to have been around forever ... all stuffed inside this little fantasy. This time it was a new one. Vivian. A stunning little blonde. Maybe twenty-two ... twenty-three years old.

Fascinating. Yes. The little process of talking and chatting. She asks my name, what I do, have I ever been in there before. And then at some point we both agree on a certain song she will dance to, and then she gets up and makes room for herself and stands in front of me and looks down rather naughtily and begins removing her clothing and placing it on the back of her chair until she is wearing only a T-back bikini bottom.

I sit down in the chair, taking her all in. It's somewhat ridiculous. She begins swaying her hips with her mouth slightly open and squeezing her breasts carefully and caressing them and looking down at them. Then she closes in on the side of her face with her forearm, which she bites for a second before opening her eyes to me and turning around to display her ass. Yes. The ass. A sort of painting, no ... a sculpture, yes ... a sculpture ... a collection of matter ... courtesy of the earth ... courtesy of the epochs ... courtesy of the cosmos.

It's all so hilarious. People all around. The music is blaring. All the lights and the smoke. You're out in public, but it doesn't matter. Neither of you are acknowledging any of this whatsoever. Both of you could be alone in a side room of some castle chamber far underground for all you act like.

Yes. Vivian was the type that would reach back and (with her head to the side) smile and grind her haunches slightly and lovingly upon you.

At this point, there is a sort of focused awe and fascination. Especially if you're already high. You don't even really want to touch her. Or if so, only slightly. Yes. You're too intoxicated. A dreamy, moonlike bliss settles over you. Fleshy and captivating and final. You only want her to keep on dancing forever, to melt into her curvy feminine glow.

For a few minutes there is a lack of concept or time, but eventually the song will end and she will stop dancing and there is the twenty to worry about. You sit back up in your chair and reach for your wallet as she puts her clothes back on. It's almost like sex, only you're sitting in a club.

I place the bill inside her bikini on the top side of her hips. She laughs, asks if I enjoyed her dancing. We light up cigarettes, start talking. Soon I purchase another dance. On it goes. All evening. Little episodes of her stripping and squirming around and then putting her clothes back on, and then the next cigarette comes out, and finally we just sit back and drink and watch the crowd and the rest of the girls.

All these shapes and bodies moving around you. Walking past here. Bending over there. Onstage here. Stepping down there. All lounging and strutting around all night long.

Another hour or so and eventually it's closing time. Everything changes all of a sudden. All the lights go on. The spell is broken. Everything looks suddenly normal, un-enchanting, slightly drab. Waitresses begin scurrying around. Bar staff begin to clean up. The girls are called away to the dressing room. Vivian and I get up and say goodnight until next time, and then I shuffle out with the rest of them.

And then walking down the street afterward. Happy. Drunk. Up ahead the late-night scene. A police threesome. Walking. Walking. Slight paranoia. Feigned nonchalance. Finally past. Drifting back to my waiting sportster. Faded red. Mellow. Faithful. I insert a drunken key. We laugh and make off.

6

▼

Thursday. 12:03 am.

I'm sitting here pouring wine. Another week has passed. Maybe two. I've run out of money. Imagine! The Wheel that never stops has forced me to find employment again. In this case, a semiconductor/computer-chip equipment supplier. Evening shift. Naturally. Compliments of "Yesterdays Temporary Service."

I've been in this high-tech maze for months now. Working, not working, working. It's all I know.

I've decided all I really want to do in life is just sit like this and type forever, periodically interrupted only by Rachel. Yes.

My own personal off-and-on lay, Libby, bores me. I will tell you more about her later. Maybe. I used to work with her. We started talking. She comes over now every month or so just to spite her husband. It's absurd.

I'm pouring more wine now. My life has become days and days of work. Again. I cannot earn money except at the cost of myself. And always inside a big, sterile, gray manufacturing nightmare. I should be grateful, but I'm not. I can't help it.

But wait ... ssshh ... listen. Here it is. Last night I found the meaning of everything ...

7

▼

WEDNESDAY. 1:01 PM.

Mmm. Meanwhile I drift into work. This is what I do when not engaged in reading and thinking and typing and going to The Lady. It's sickening. I do it every day now. Winding down the streets and out onto the freeway for a few minutes and then down the Highway 290 extension and out to a huge assemblage of boxy, boring, computerized abortions. With offices and parking lots and ventilation structures and thousands of cars and concrete and little trees and curbs and attempts at landscaping. Little patches and strips of green here and there, all a sprawling, bloated spectacle of dullness and death. A spiritual wasteland.

I park, walk in ... flash my badge. Soon I am down a long hall and turning into a gowning area. It is usually crowded. We slip on our little suits over our clothing. Our little white space suits. Mustn't get any contaminants on the product! Oh no! That wouldn't do at all! That's a quality issue! We have regulations ... and protocol! It's global now!

I zip up my jumpsuit, slip on my booties, tie my hood down ... walk over near the laundry bin, pop my surgeon's gloves on, and then a quick check in the mirror. I am little space boy. Galaxy Mining Company. Late 28th century. A Martian slave. Species: human. Life expectancy: fifty years. Favorite thoughts: none. Ambition: "Only to work, sir."

I venture forth into a different world. I walk through a passageway and ventilation system and through a small corridor and out onto "the floor."

Immediately there is the NASA-like drone of machinery being tested and the sound of voices and the sight of odd little tools and air guns and wires. The sight of heating units and oxygen chambers and laser guns and nitrogen containers and electrical outlets, and tool chests with all manner of nuts and bolts and wrenches and sockets and screws and adaptors and blades and screwdrivers and taps and little hammers and gauges and glue and tape and foam and inserts.

Out on the floor there are a dozen machine frames (approximately five by five feet) upon each of which sits an odd collection of wiring and conduit boxes and fat, watermelon-shaped gas chambers connected with thin networks of weldments and lines and gauges and mass-flow controllers and valves and gaskets and readouts. Peculiar, specialized little affairs, all in various stages of evolution and completion and assimilation.

I walk back to my area ... my little table surrounded by four or five of my little companions and supervisors and engineers. Yes. I am the temporary. The hired help. I am responsible for completing the shitty, difficult little tasks that nobody else wants to do. It is the natural way. Everybody does it. It's the free-trade agreements. And then when necessary we're out with the laundry.

We stand around for a few minutes at the beginning of every shift ... everyone looking somewhat preposterous in their white little outfits. Their "smocks," as they call them. It took me a few days to get used to it. My superiors are both Indian. Sometimes when they are having a spat they start jabbering in Hindi. It is fascinating. These little sounds ... leaping softly from their dark lips. Then they catch themselves, return to English, apologize.

But I have developed a certain affection for the one. One R.D. Rhanivasan. His degree clashes with his personality. A PhD in mechanical engineering. He comes from money. Thirty-four years old. Super-fluent English. Kind. Charming. Slightly British. Beautiful wife. A soft gentle personality, upper class, with a capacity for suffering and an awareness of situation.

He spends most of his time drawing up solutions to various engineering problems as relate to weldment design, system configuration, etc. He frequently delegates authority to the younger, more ambitious of the two, one Dankhar Singh. Dankhar loves everything. He loves work, loves the company, loves problems, loves deadlines, loves machines, loves computers, loves weldments, loves engineering, loves gadgets, loves technicality, loves loving. Perfect for the job.

But what they get me to take care of most of the time is insulating the weldments, the small cylindrical metal tubes that transport gases from the deposition chamber of the machine to the gas panel. The first few days it was slightly interesting. It requires a certain art, a certain dexterity and strength of forearm. All in all very delicate and time-consuming. Yes. The gas must stay heated to a certain temperature, so as not to condensate and come dripping out onto the microchip at the other end up inside the gas chamber and ruining it. Then later on there is the installation of the gas panel and mass-flow controllers and the attaching of weldments to the chambers with nuts and bolts and gaskets and heat sensors and the elimination of any gas leaks. A few weeks and a few million dollars later, and *voila*—an ion implanter! Let the microchips flow!

And so there I sit. Every night. Perfecting my little method. I attach the heater cable to the weldment and secure it with zip wrapping and close up the insulation with my right hand and then gradually work my left hand over it, looping and revolving the roll over and around and back down the other side, overlapping each layer upon the one previous. The effect is like the red stripes on a candy cane, except much closer together. And gray.

And then two hours and some sweat later, when you are finished with it and it is time to install it, you almost look at it with a certain fondness, but then you are quickly called to take it away to the monster that needs it and begin the next task.

And so it is. Every afternoon. Five or six times a week. Five or six episodes of me and the engineers and our never-ending little supply of X-3000s, with their constant buzzing need of tinkering and adjustment and configuration and panels and lines and chambers.

On it goes. Every day now. It's ridiculous. I should be grateful.

8

▼

THURSDAY. 1:30 AM.

Last night I lucked upon a delicious dinner … gratis from Aaron. Aaron the Mystic. Yes. West Lynn Cafe. This lifted my spirits considerably. But as usual, I had to sit there and listen to all his spiritual hocus pocus. Yes. He fills my head with karma till it overflows. Conversation so heavy I must order a side of rice to carry on. Plenty of sauce, that's what I say! Yes, yes. *I love it.*

We're sitting there stuffing our gut with some kind of Tandoori curry … from some Indian hearth somewhere … I'm off on a tangent about something … tearing off a piece of bread … chewing … chewing physics and cosmology … chewing humans and psychology and money and automation … chewing nothing ever ends … and laughing. And then here Aaron comes …

"Well you know, Gerald … according to the Master … this world doesn't even really exist … we think this world exists because of our five senses … our senses distort our reality … "

I dip my bread. My jaws are going up and down happily.

"If we learn to focus our attention, Gerald … through the grace and guidance of the perfect, living Master … then we can one day return to our Source … our true Home. But meditation, meditation is the key."

I'm sitting there with my bread … looking at him. Fascinating. Yes, but he has an ability to process and appreciate quirks and subtleties of all kinds. And he hacks away at his own little houses in his mind. And he's always there. Yes. He tends to his own shit. And with a sense of humor. This is so rare in our world.

I tear off some more bread, reach over for the olive oil.

"I meditated last night … in the bathroom."

Aaron almost spills his herbal tea, has to reach over for his napkin. We both cackle out laughing.

"And I had an out-of-body experience too. But it went down the drain."

Now I have to reach for my napkin. There is a slight commotion at the table. Laughter. The owner comes over to ask if everything is all right. Susan. She's about thirty-eight. Brunette. Thin. Attractive. She's always looking at us. I can tell Aaron secretly wants her.

She walks back off. We're still laughing. Slowly we get it together.

"Gerald, now, were you concentrating on a certain form when you had your out of body experience?"

Another outburst, more commotion. We need new napkins. Susan glances over continually.

We get it together again.

"Yes, yes."

I have the coffee cup up to my lips.

"It was very radiant. And I was repeating the image in my mind."

Aaron sips his tea.

"Could you feel the sweet Nectar of Wisdom rising up within you?"

She kicks us out at this last outburst. We have to continue on at his nice big house on 46th Street.

Yes … he confessed his continual lust for women despite his efforts at meditation. I wanted to fall on the floor laughing. I couldn't stop. On and on. I wanted to kiss him.

It seems a young *nurse* has caught his eye. Imagine that! And in a hospital! Good God! No more merging with the Absolute! Oh no … never … he's finished! *Finis*! He'll come back as a frog … 1,700 times … without a doubt! And no water either!

9

▼

SATURDAY. 5:07 PM.

I am down to days and weeks again. I am down to nothing. There is only food and other intoxicants. I see everything all around me. I know how it has to be done now. Ghosts, chips, antimatter, carvings, works of art, ways of doing, the dirt of life, poems, restaurants, bacchanalia, vice, victory, volume.

I laugh hideously. I shake my head. I defy everything. I follow something resembling a thought down a long black hall with a large whip in my hand. I chase it out, and we laugh together.

And last night, a play. Yes. I took off early from the bastard job. Yes. Kian ... Irish boy, made his little debut at Zachary Scott Theatre. It's at Barton Springs and Lamar Boulevard. A cozy place. Small. Dark.

Yes. I walk in, find a seat. The lights go down. I sit there. Slightly inebriated. Pleasant. Hopeful. The curtain draws.

It is a comedy. Russia. Nineteenth century. The czars are still riding high. The young protagonist, Boris, spends his time needling his way into the good graces of a middle-class family. How could he stand them! And he couldn't! Immature little half spirits. Full of superstition and hypocrisy and banality.

And Kian: sitting there onstage, a subordinate schemer … with an angle of his own. Dreaming culture and operas. Dreaming silly fat wives with large bank accounts. He lounges on the couch with a large milk cow … dressed in pearls and lace and fanning herself. I take it all in. I study him closely. Then he comes out with it. Fires up the stage with a large bellow of dedication and affirmation.

And then he pulls it off: he plants a large wet one square on her fat, pink lips and she is gasping and moaning and fanning herself as the curtain closes. A massive success.

And afterwards, drinks and merriment and introductions, and then he and I continuing on at his large sprawling suburban affair that he shares with Seth, a young student, and Gurney, a dog lover.

They are out. Quickly we fill the room. Soon candles and cha cha a Latino. Soon tea and marijuana a la mode. And Kian … Kian the Irish … spewing forth suddenly … a celebratory spew of science-fiction brew … yes, yes, he launches forth suddenly in time to the music … he veers all over the highway. I am smoking and sitting on the edge of my cushion, leaning forward, giggling, snickering, yes, yes, in encouragement, and he trails off and I pick it up and shake it and get on for a ride … a ride to wherever … wherever it goes … and it is an orgasm of impersonations and humor and insolence, and he grabs the reins from me again and not to be outdone, he stands up suddenly on the couch and steps onto the coffee table, all the while unsheathing his mental Irish member, and he proceeds to empty his cranium off all over the floor about everything of note or absurdity or hypocrisy that he's ever seen or heard or imagined as I am rolling and gasping and falling off my chair, where I hold my stomach and heave for some odd minutes more.

And then we are up at the kitchen table, where we dig out some bread and cheese and strawberries from the refrigerator and soon we are giggling and trailing off and stuffing these strange, high, tasty little chunks and portions and wet red breasts of matter into our mouths, with Kian snickering back and forth in between swallows with his green, Irish little accent …

"You know, Gerald … I must say … "

Then, catching the sound of his own ridiculous voice, he mocks his own words in a fake Southern accent.

"You know, Gerald ... I must say ... "
Then equally in female soprano ... from Georgia:
"You know, Gerald ... I must say ... "
And then, Italian:
"You know, Gerald ... I must say ... "
And then he's off ...
London ... upper class:
"You know, Gerald ... I must say ... "
French:
"You know, Gerald ... I must say ... "
German:
"You know, Gerald ... I must say ... "

I look off, as he's talking ... light a cigarette ... launch off into a little introductory monologue ...
"Ladies and gentleman ... yes, welcome ... yes ... Ladies and gentleman ... yes, thank you ... thank you ... yes ladies and gentleman, a very special, special surprise tonight ... "

Scottish sheepherder ... standing in the rain:
"You know, Gerald ... I must say ... "
Gesturing homosexual:
"You know, Gerald ... I must say ... "

"Yes, ladies and gentleman ... a very warm welcome ... I present to you ... a man who needs no introduction ... Ladies and gentleman ... a man known on the circuit ... since the beginning ..."

British rock-and-roll musician, smoking a cigarette:
"You know, Gerald ... I must say ... "
California hippie ... stoned:
"You know, Gerald ... I must say ... "

" ... yes ... since the beginning ... I ... I remember our first crowd ... it was such a very, very fine night ... I'm recalling it now ... we were ... we were floating in booze ... it was ... really, really special ... I remember ... I ... well, I don't remember anything really ... it was ... really a very fine night ... and ... "

Opera singer, baritone:

"You know, Gerald ... I mu-uust say ... "
Boxing announcer, radio ... 1940's:
"You know, Gerald ... I must say ... "

" ... and ... and the whole place really ... even the tables were floating ... well ... I don't really remember anything about the tables ... but we were floating ... all of us ... I ... I know I was ... "

Sweaty, sports post-interview, Brooklyn:
"You know, Gerald ... I must say ... "

" ... and ... and it seemed everyone was ... well ... I know ... I know my wife was floating ... yes ... or at least she looked liked she was floating ... or maybe she had been floating ... in any case she ... *should have been* floating ... yes ... she *should have been* floating ... and ... and *floating* ... and ... I'm beginning to float right now actually ... or at least ... I ... *seem* to be floating ... "

Horse-racing announcer:
"You know, Gerald ... I must say ... "
Computerized, android:
"You know, Gerald ... I must say ... "

"In fact, I ... I sometimes ... I sometimes tend to ... to float right off ... I think I might just float off right now actually ... and ... and we'll just ... we'll just sort of ... float right on off ... there now ... together, like ... yes that's it ... just ... just float right on off ... "

Unintelligible:
"You know, Gerald ... I must say ... "
Unintelligible again:
"You know, Gerald ... I must say ... "

10

▼

TUESDAY. 1:48 AM.

I return to my room, look around, wait for the days to slip by. I sense this particular job will be over soon. Another two or three weeks. I can read between the lines of our pathetic memos. There seems to be a lull in demand. Yes. Soon it'll be no more ridiculous white suits. No more clean-room etiquette. No more wrenches and ratchets and weldments. No more carts and levers and screwdrivers. No more tape and scissors and razor blades and readouts and isopropanol and drills and taps and flow controllers and helium leaks and ground cables and conduit boxes and nitrogen and argon and plasma fields and pneumatic valves. No more poly lines and heater guns and vapor deposition and tungsten purges and bubble tests and step-four diagnostics. No more, no more, no more!

And perfect timing. Yes. You see, a screw popped loose tonight in my head. I fell apart at work. My poor Hindu co-workers had never seen this. I went off on them. Yes ... right in the middle of turning a wrench on one of the X-3000s. I let loose a miniature tirade on that hazy entity called "The Customer" that was always draped over our heads. I rambled on and on ... invective here and there ... finally lapsing into silence.

A few seconds passed. I felt like I had spilled my drink and needed a napkin.

And Dankhar … the engineer … the technical guru … the rudder of the shift, suddenly pipes up.

Yes … Dankhar—intelligent, but quite dumb somehow. Amazing how he does it. I've learned he's a genius in that respect. Remarkable! Yes, he comes to life with a small lecture on the usefulness of the concept … the advantages … the functionality.

Ah, my God! As if I wasn't raised on juicy American steak such as this! I wanted to laugh. It was good. A lecture by Dankhar about The Customer! But my mouth was zipped tight. I quickly agreed to inhibit his flow. I couldn't take any more. I started feeling lightheaded. Finally he abandoned it. He was right, actually.

The shift passed.

II

▼

SUNDAY. 3:06 PM.

The job has ended! Yes! We were let go finally. My assignment is over. A little yellow slip, and off you go! I'm lying here in bed now, still stunned and delighted. All I have to do now is float through the days.

And last night Morton and I celebrated at Les Amis. A Saturday. Yes. Everything quite beautiful. All the world a giant museum. Made for your touching and interacting pleasure. Invitations scattered at random entrances:

"Please touch and seek after pleasure, but do so at your own risk. Some creatures are alive and forming."

And we entered. Borrowing a light and some sweetener for starters. A threesome at the table next to us. High cheekbones. Slightly European. Smoking casually. Yes. A slight overture at mingling. A gesture at fusion. A few words and a smile. An acknowledgment of possibility. Two tables considering each other like entrees. Sources of pleasure and fuel. All accomplished by a simple request. Chosen as a result of situation. A reason for interaction and possible creation.

We smile, turn back around, take it all in.

And then, conversation erupting between us. Perceptions of existence relative to position. Relative to view. The mind-altering correctness of everything. The genius of circumstance. The capacity for self-destruction. The horror and simultaneous beauty of it all. All the forces of nature, lurking in varying degrees in all of us.

All the unknowns, the death, the days in the sun. All the money, the information, the days. The technology! The beginnings. The ends. The rat race! The pop culture! The nonstop bullshit!

We ended up at The Lady.

12

▼

FRIDAY. 3:01 PM.

I sit down at my typewriter, look out the window.

The sky has cleared. Yes. It has stormed tremendously, and there are limbs and trees and bits of swirl and leftover madness everywhere. All in the driveway. All on the sidewalk. Bits and pieces of things strewn all over the lawn. It happens like this in my head as well.

Bicyclers begin to coast by in their little suits of yellow and black. All the cars sit contentedly up and down the street, their engines drifting off in the late afternoon. Some will be roused from their slumber later on. The key is their master. Off they'll go! Belching fumes, disgruntled, hungry for gas and oil ... forced to shuffle their mad owners off to some evening rendezvous ... to the grocery store, to the bar, to the late movie, to a coffee house, to a house of shame, to an edge ... out and beyond and back again.

Wait. There is a strange noise now in the other apartment ...

(I go listen for a second, walk back over and sit down again.)

It has been vacant for a while. A young Marine sergeant and his wife were making a go of it, and then one day out of the blue she up and leaves him. Yes. Her car had been gone for a while. He stopped me out in the yard one day as I was walking up. Long face, sad crew cut, tattoos sagging. I didn't even have to ask. I felt bad for him. He was a nice sort actually. At any rate, he was out too in a few more days.

I immediately took to sitting on their front porch in the early afternoons. I still wasn't working. There was a large sign out in the grass advertising the room. People started coming by in droves … everyone … every day. I started fielding questions like I owned the place. It seemed everybody was just dying to move in there.

"Oh, we just love Hyde Park."

Claptrap like that. Naturally, the better looking the young Ms., the more I juiced the place up.

"Oh yes, a lovely neighborhood. No, no … I'm sure you could get him down cheaper than that … oh yes, you'd love it here."

I was sick of college students, though. With their shitty beer and their business dreams. And the fraternities. Sigma Phi Suck … and the Beta Money Kappas … yes.

For one of these, the price automatically doubled.

"Oh yes … I'm trying to move out myself. The landlord's an ass … and he's fat … and he threatens eviction quite regularly … he likes the rent to be in his greasy little hands right on the first … and no later! Not a day … not an hour … not a second!"

I thought my little scheme was working. It seemed at least three little hotties were aching to move in. But then … much to my horror … I see the car pull up the driveway … Augh! It couldn't be! But it was. I never did figure out what happened. Some blond kid from Pennsylvania. Christ! Where were the women? Why not a nice little exchange student from Sweden … or a cello player … or an antique collector … or a waitress … with common sense and a good figure.

13

▼

WEDNESDAY. 7:49 PM.

One day out of boredom I decide to visit the music center down at the university and try to find a cheap piano recital by one of the aspiring little composers. Yes.

I amble down there. A good twenty or thirty minutes through Hyde Park and over to Guadalupe Street. I wander past the buildings and into the famous hall, mill about out in the lobby.

Yes. Hmm. And it seems a practice has just ended. Yes. I look around. A horde of little musical princesses exits a practice room down the hall from the lobby. You know the kind. Ah, they've seen me lurking around before. They turn away. Little whores! I walk up to take a closer look at them, glancing at a schedule of events as a decoy. Hmmm ... let's see ... Chopin on Wednesday by a young Asian girl of nineteen ... oh that's at seven ... I won't make it ... am due at a reception ... hmmm ... Rachmaninoff tomorrow afternoon, performed by a young blond boy who is no doubt much more acquainted with these girls than I will ever be.

Suddenly I am aware of myself. I look over at them. How dainty and cruel they are! Sitting around on sofas and velvetries with their flutes and their papers and their laughter. A little circle of vicious cherubs ... each on their own merciless cloud ... floating sublimely through a fake heaven. The young Rachmaninoff quickly trots over like a jealous little stallion, rump flared out like he's about to shit some music ... he prances up ... proceeds to stake his claim, necking and rubbing and greeting ... meanwhile eyeing me ... making sure I knew they were off limits ... making sure I knew they all belonged to his symphonic harem.

And they did. All of them vying for his attention. Little music boxes they were ... needing only to be wound up. And it seemed he did it. And together they formed a sort of orchestra. And they played for me. Yes ... an orchestra ... playing works of conversation to a hall nearly empty. He began to conduct them, giving each one the lead as she wanted it. I watched them with a strange mixture of disgust, fascination, and affection. They were very young. Somewhat talented. Idealistic still. Ridiculous. Polished. Very polished.

But there was no reaching these. It was impossible. They were under lock and key. A lock and key that required some strange little code.

And only Rachmaninoff had it.

14

▼

FRIDAY AND WINE.

It's almost midnight. I'm sitting here thinking of summers past … to that summer when Jens and I quit our jobs and purchased plane tickets to Europe. Those were the days, then. Yes. And how we landed and eventually made our way down Spain to Morocco and to a bar the one night in Casablanca.

Yes. Casablanca. An armpit of a city with a romantic name.

Yes. I remember this prostitute there thought I was going to take her back to the U.S. and marry her. She assumed this from what our "associates" at the bar had told her. The Moroccans. And I never even touched her except for a bit of fondling. She was asking way too much. Five hundred dollars for the night. Ridiculous.

Yes. Jens and myself, sitting at a bar in Casablanca. Very high on hashish. Something out of a *Star Wars* bar scene. Everything insane. You just look around and go with it. You reach a point where finally you just sit back and let come what may.

Strange characters sitting around … looking at you … staring at you … A'rabs … businessmen, people out for the night. It's all smoke and madness and drinks coming around and people shuffling by and laughing and hubbub. All these faces … tan and unshaven and laughing. White teeth and big throaty laughs, and we just sat there. Everything surreal. Hashish smoke. Cigarette smoke. Every single person smoking and drinking. Bottles were taken away and someone looks at you and sits down and new bottles are brought ... never mind who ordered them, and you are all on instinct and going with it and fascinated by it and sensing that absolutely anything could happen at any particular moment and something is said at the table next to us and suddenly someone slaps his date in the face a bit and I look off for a second and then back over there and she is jerking him by the collar and shaking him and screaming obscenities.

Finally she lets him back down ... still hissing. He leans over to our table and tries to start speaking to me in Arabic. I look off. It flies from his mouth. Little bits of machine-gun fire. He seems to be getting agitated. I look at him, shake my head, make a motion with my hand ... put it to my mouth.

"Sorry, my friend ... English? Do you speak English? ... Aung-lees ... "

No English. He's still jabbering. Gesturing. Finally I blurt out my thimbleful of Arabic.

"*Makim Mushkin* ... hey *Makim Mushkin* ... "

His date brightens up at this.

"Ah ... *Makim Mushkin* ... "

She turns to him ... scolds him for making me feel uncomfortable. He looks back over, nods strangely ... stares a bit ... shakes his head up and down. She recognizes the situation, smiles coyly. They are amused at my effort. Eventually, they resume their babble.

Hash joints are being rolled and a strange, snaky music is crawling through our heads and everything is gone, gone. The vulnerability is overwhelming ... the intensity is overwhelming and you have no idea about the passage of time and it is far from your mind and everything is a dream reel playing out ... and I would look around ... into their faces, say ... a few couples ... or a man sitting at a table, and the year becomes 1911 ... or 786 ... and the United States doesn't exist yet. And they look at you and it is a face from somewhere else ... a glance from somewhere else. Then a cigarette is lit and more beer is brought and many are high and you are very high and you smirk approvingly ... operating now from a different point of reference. Laughing and playing with reality and trying to stay sane and in your chair and not let it all force you into the madhouse ...

And then the waiter comes over and gives this sly smile and you cannot even grasp what's going on and you drink your beer and it tastes very sweet and superb and you cannot imagine why this beer tastes so good and you look at the bottle and smack your lips and smile and look up and laugh again for no reason and you feel it as you swallow go all the way down to your stomach.

Then somewhere along the way a woman of about thirty-two is sitting beside me, with black hair and a good figure, and she's wearing some sort of native robe and she keeps trying to hold my hand. She had spotted us from a ways off and our Moroccan "friends" we had met had motioned her over and suddenly she is sitting there beside me.

I look across at Jens ... laughing his fool head off. There is a face, an attractive, dark, strange female face ... twenty inches from mine, staring ... and I look over at her and kept looking and looking and finally she became real to me ... something tangible and a woman. Yes, a woman sitting there very close to me ... not speaking any English ... not knowing me ... somewhat of a prostitute ... yet laughing with her friend and holding my strange little hand. Suddenly it was the thing to do. Yes, of course. Sit here and hold this woman's hand. It was something I could touch and feel, and it didn't go away.

She kept speaking Arabic to other tables ... motioning to me ... smiling ... her little idiot prince. She finds out quickly from our friends that we are American. They would talk and I would look at her and she would stop talking and look at me and smile. Gradually we began to communicate through gestures and facial expressions. Yes. Her holding my right hand between her two lovely dark ones, and I am drinking and extremely high and we are communicating through gestures. There was nothing to my existence, past or future, except that particular moment. I kept looking off and laughing, and she would pinch me slightly and smile and say "what?" with her eyebrows. And then I would assure her with my eyes that nothing was the matter, and she would motion to the hash and smile and shake her head "yes?" And I would say "yes" with my face ... yes, that's it, honey. And then she laughs and shows off her perfect angel white teeth and they were the whitest teeth I had ever seen.

Soon my princess and I developed a language of nods and complex pushes and curvings of the eyebrows and hand motions and smiles and various other newfound means of communication, and finally when some hard-to-get-across point had made the journey and we both realized it, it was like we had created something completely new for ourselves and we became elated once more and just sat and looked at each other, smiling and laughing, and presently I reach over and put my hand on the side of her face and her mouth is moist and we engage in a slow searching kiss.

I pull away presently. I felt the whole planet must surely be high. Everyone, everywhere basking and rolling around in dopamine euphoria. With something pretty to touch ... whenever they want.

I erupt again into a spasm of delight. Laughing at the whole thing. Laughing at her. Laughing at myself. Laughing at existence. We were peaking in several different areas.

This went on for some time, and finally we all got up and walked across the street to another bar. Jens and I dished out about thirty dollars American for a bottle of the most expensive whiskey in the house. It was gone in about an hour.

Finally at about 4:00 AM it all ended. Our "friends" told the woman that I would take her back to the United States. She kept trying to say she loved me in English. She looked at me nodding her head "yes?" and smiling. I nodded my head "yes" and our lips found each other again. I was supposed to meet her again the next day at some predetermined place set up by the friends. They told me I should give her some money for that night's company. Money? Sure, what's money. I gave her a wad of several hundred dirham. About fifty dollars American. She thought I was loaded.

Drunk, still somewhat high and no taxis around. We walked through various back streets and alleyways. Wandering. The middle of the night. Music spilling out every once in a while from somewhere. Dogs barking. Curly, snaky, strange lettering everywhere. Laughing occasionally. I had no idea who I was. Just going with it. A night of nights. Smoking cigarettes. Ambling along. I wasn't even walking. More like floating through a sequence or a dream. A nonentity. A molecule. A cloud. A few hours passing like seconds. Seconds taking up a few hours.

*   *   *   *

Yes ... I care not that I have never found a woman I could love eternally. This is mere piffle. What is eternal???? ... Nothing. This realization is eternal. What do I care for love? I love feeling, ardor, sensation, the ephemeral jewel. All things transitory. Passion is what creates. Passion of all kinds. Smoky, fiery passion. With ashes and embers in its wake. To be passionate is to be immortal. Love will give perception and background and comfort. But passion is the king. The lonely creator. The original drug.

I am full of fire. My body trembles. I bite my hands. Madness consumes me. I think of the universe. Continuing on. Ad infinitum! With or without you. But for a little while, with you! The very idea! Titillating! I am intoxicated by it. I dream crazily. At all hours. The day ... another dream ... Les Amis ... not even there, still dreaming. Everything is mixed. Surreal. I think of all the stories, all the Greek gods and goddesses. Their fervor, their frailty, their creations. Their folly. Their perversions. Their incest, their ideals. Their power, their wisdom.

Everything is delicious and silly. I marvel at simplicity. And chaos. The great wonder. Rendering everything relative, laughable. Yes. I wish I could sex all the great women of the world. I think of Lady Godiva. Joan of Arc. Pocahontas. Sophia Loren. Barbara Eden. Brigitte Bardot. Ava Gardner. Raquel Welch.

Cleopatra!

The Virgin Mary!

... Eve!!!

... *God*!!!!!!!!

PART 2

▼

I

▼

SUNDAY. 3:21 PM.

It's been a month or so. I can't tell what has happened. Nothing has happened.

Wait a second ... my cigarette has gone out. There we are. Mmm. I am sick, but healthy. Everyone around me is pissing music. The little virtuoso in the back room ... grinding away on his violin ... ow! A wrong note!

I'm looking around for something to throw.

Where was I? Oh yes ... Morton. He's sweating over his latest scheme. He does this from time to time. Lately it's been supplying flood-zone data to mortgage-hungry banks and various credit unions. He fancies himself a sort of information broker. And so he is! He's even pulled in a bit of money over the phone. We go and buy some cheap red and toast his success. He marvels at how easy it was. "Even you could do it." Yes.

You should see the enthusiasm he has for these little ploys. He wants it to get bigger. His eyes twinkle. Yes. He wants employees! Computers! Trips! He goes on and on and on.

I leave him to it.

Meanwhile, I sit down here. The moon is in a new phase. I come out only at night now. I have been running low. I seldom see anyone anymore. I don't work. I have a little bit of money in the bank. Everything is perfect.

2

▼

Monday.

The university comes to life. I couldn't care less. I look off. Sneeze. Go masturbate.

3

▼

TUESDAY.

A dull, banal Tuesday. I'll have to stop typing soon and look for work. I'm getting low. Everything is crashing. And I want it to. Oh yes! I want it to crash and burn. The harder the better. Here we go. This will be one to remember. I am looking around at the scenery as I go by.

I am laughing. Oh shit, shit. But won't you kindly step inside? You won't regret it! I'll explain it all to you. I won't leave you by yourself. You'll have your heart's desire. And I, mine. Come, come ...

6:00 PM.

I climb back in my chair. Once again I am not looking for anything.

Now listen. I only want what I know, and that is getting to be less and less. I pour everything out and stand looking at the bottom of the glass. Life is not short. Life is long and sprinkled with senselessness and mild brutality. I have fish eyes and am lying in the grass of everywhere. Split days are what I do. Near miss and gutter wind. Horrible at times, but not altogether tragic.

You see, contradiction is the key. Life is a contradiction. Life is honest. Many things aren't even definable, at least not in our present languages. And life, in its best moments, whether they be gray or flashing or cold or cruel, is at the very least unaffected and timeless, with a genius of its own.

But! Oh yes ... but, but ... *but*! I have the key, you see ... the trump card ... the irrational magic wand now ... and that is ... the mother of all blessings ... I have it now: *disinterest*! Oh yes! Disinterest ... and *imagination*! Ha! There you are. *Ha! Ha! Ha!* Yes, who could believe it. But, there it is ... oh yes! The dynamic duo: disinterest and imagination. Oh ho! Oh my!

Essentially, it is this. I am running just ahead of poverty's jaws. I wouldn't care except the phone keeps ringing. I will not go anywhere today. I know how it is done. I am preoccupied with nothingness. I wish for nothing. And no heaven either.

You see, this is my heaven. My heaven and hell. It's all the same. Whatever key you fish out of your pocket automatically transforms the intended room into the thought. The thought unlocks the door and the room becomes the expectation. You walk in, puzzled at first, and then slowly start to mold the sights and sounds to fit your new perspective. Yes! In the end, we are all artists! Yes! We all sculpt ourselves to fit the never-ending advance of circumstance! Circumstance! Circumstance!

4

▼

Tuesday. 9:18 pm.

Such things weren't on my mind last night, however. No. I was too busy enjoying the company of one well-proportioned, redheaded little fox. Oh, she was a talker! A talking little picture. Yes. A figurine, sitting up on a shelf, all by herself ... a little golden figurine with tiny hands curving up toward the sky and a face like an angel. I snatched her up. Not caring of the price. Ah ... yes ... I'll take ... *this*. Suddenly she came to life. As soon as I touched her. My talking little figurine. Tossing her thick red hair. Laughing, silliness. She appeared out of the past, suddenly. Still glistening. Glistening adolescent sex and shimmer. Leading me off to Town Lake. Singing. Touching. A tracing of the lips. The elixir of Night. The eyes flashing. It was all there.

5

▼

SUNDAY. 10:09 PM.

Now tonight. I turn on the radio ... eventually find PBS. There is singing. Singing some folk-dance piece ... possibly from the Appalachian region. It has, here and there, certain operatic tendencies, but never quite leaves the womb of its mountain origin.

The insane little red fireball of sex and chatter. She wouldn't like this kind of music. I am remembering my earlier conclusions about her. Only sometimes you go back to certain things in your life when nothing seems to be in front of you at that particular moment.

No, she wouldn't like this sort of music at all ... she's always changing the station or the disc ... asking if it's okay while she does it ... stretching and gazing about the room.

"Well, you know it just doesn't fit my mood ... I mean ... just ... you know ... it's okay once in a while, but I'm just not in the right mood ... see look, I know a good station ... let me just find it here ... "

Me sitting there. Watching her ... despising her ... turned on by her ... wanting to slap her a good one. She is a toy queen. Clueless. Bossy. Gliding around in her temporary little spring kingdom. I started picturing her at forty ... fifty.

Most of the time I just shut up and listen to her babble. She can't stand silence. Most women can't. They think something is wrong. She talks to keep what she imagines as the mood going. And all of it's spurts and volleys and masturbations of words. With a screamer thrown in every once in a while with some effect. All of it very bizarre and unreal, enhanced by her squirming and writhing around all over my floor, yawning and stretching into the air.

And then ...

"You think maybe you could do me a little favor ... "

She takes off her shoes.

"My feet ... they hurt a little ... you think maybe you could rub them for me ... it would feel so good ... I haven't had my feet rubbed in such a long time."

I'm sitting there ... looking at her. Amazed. Not at her request, but at the strangeness that shapes our evenings together. It's not as if I don't know that it is a classic tale of the obvious, us being the latest characters. No, I know it even as it is happening and yet somehow content myself to float through it all. Dreamy. Obliging. Agreeable. Thoughtless. In the way that a fed cat is thoughtless. I put her foot up in my lap, gripping her heel. I massage it firmly in little circles, and then up the arch, grinding in with my thumb. I take my time.

"Ooooh, that feels so good."

She's sprawled out on the floor, looking around, blinking her eyes very slowly. She's quiet for a while, to my surprise and enjoyment. I squeeze the ball of her foot, working the muscle good. Kneading it ... pushing it ... rubbing it.

"Ooooh."

Her hair is everywhere. Her body is limp. She looks like a rag. I bend all of her toes back ... over the top of her foot. Hold them there. I was half expecting her to metamorphose into another shape. That's how it is with her. You wonder where she's from. She could have transformed her own DNA pattern ... or spoken to me suddenly in an alien voice and I wouldn't have been a bit surprised.

Still she was silent. Except for an occasional moan. And finally sitting up on her elbows. Suddenly, I couldn't resist her meaty calves and thighs, since I had turned her into Jell-O. I commenced to devouring her.

Then I had a thought. Speed. She'd probably done a lot of amphetamines. Not that it mattered. I looked at her again. Her face seemed to alternate expressions. Each coming in and out of focus. There was something in her. Her mouth opened and she let out a giggle. I eased her back down to the floor.

She seemed to sleep. There were two of her, but I was moving away from both … again.

So, something gives. Something's always giving. A slow creaking and moaning and then the whole thing comes crashing down like a rotten porch. The dust settles and here we are. Something like needing a can opener and finally giving up and throwing your beautiful cherries back into the sea.

6

▼

FRIDAY. 4:08 PM.

Yes, here we are. I can't tell what time it is from here. I'll be making a trip tomorrow to an old job. I've got someone there. The same absurd story. I am aching and delirious and have finally slipped down to calling up women that think I have something. Yes. Libby. My off-and-on lay. We'll sit there, talk … I'll let her feel me up. Goddamn it. It is all banal and obvious and old, but a man must eat and sleep somewhere. I'll stop writing any day now. This typewriter may be going in the next few days. Little musical fat boy is calling about the rent. It is all sickening, and I am in for a long gut-wringer of a ride. I'll meet her around 2:00 PM if I can. Her husband … fuck her husband. If he kills me, I'll just be gone. It'll all make some tiny tragic little story sometime. Maybe.

I can't get a call back about a job. I will stop typing any second now and go to bed. I should have been working again by now. I call the temporary office every day. The administrative assistant sighs when she hears my voice. Stupid whore. And I am trying to avoid the fat landlord. Oh, the banality of it all. Money, money, money. I am mentally constipated. I am immovable. I still shit away precious thoughts on beautiful strumpets. They think I am a fool? Fine, fine, let them think whatever they please. If I am, I am.

Yes … I want to be nothing! Less than nothing … sub-nothing. And I am succeeding wonderfully! Everything I want is coming true. I am pale and wasted and sick and shameless and laughing and fit only for a set of steps where I can sit down and revel in my good fortune. I boast to the air. I have invented a new style. My book is inches thick. It is full of blank pages. That is why it is so good. It is invisible. A supernova that has collapsed. Imploded. Its density has caused it to change forms. I can bend light, time, anything.

The one … Canyon. A dancer. I would like to swim laps in her deep, delicious pussy. I can't help it. I've come to the conclusion that something is wrong with me. She has the mind of a typical alcoholic pillhead, but she is of course tough somehow, somewhere. Young and talking and rubbing her magical round ass on my sleepy, curious, semi-excited member. I am led off to the execution chamber … quite willingly. Like I said, something is wrong with me. I empty my pockets and then have to beg for food. I want to lay my tired head in her lap and go to sleep. I want her to shut up. I want to talk to her. But it is impossible, you see. Something has happened.

The difference is … I have given up. The difference is … people want interest. People want you to play the game. Girls especially want you to play the game. But I can't always perform. I play a different game. I heave and ho in makeshift fountains. My sail is torn! And there is no destination!

7

▼

SUNDAY. 3:38 PM.

There is another one. Faith. Faith with the tan, butterfly beauty. Yes. She is a student. Her specialty is law, environment, etc. Somewhat intelligent. Very opinionated. Comes from money. Very easy on the eyes. A friend of Morton's. He keeps sending her my way. He was curious of the outcome. Well, here it is!

Yes. She came over this morning, didn't even sit down. I knew something was up. I could tell by the somber, condemning look she had on her face. Such a lovely face she has, this Faith ... even when she is about to kill you ... you'd let her kill you ... want her to kill you, just so you could have the eternal image of her soft sun-kissed face smoldering in your head before you go.

And kill me she has! Oh yes ... at least temporarily. Murdered in broad daylight! But I will not stay dead for long. You see, I am getting immune to death. I come from a distant line of German Frankensteins. I can lay on the table stone cold for hours, days, years! But then, presto! One miraculous, black, stormy night ... a jagged bolt of light splits the sky ... Aughhh! And I am knocked upright ... I fall off the table ... glass everywhere ... I stagger off ... the rain coming in through the roof. I look up momentarily, and then stumble down a long stone hall.

Groaning ecstatically. Alive! Alive again! And soon I am out in the deserted wet streets moaning and wailing and hideously happy.

After a few days I will heal and start speaking English again. I have two languages. English and Animal.

I look down at my chest where the bullet hole is. She only shot me once. A small caliber: .22 or so ... a little stump of a pistol. It had a queer effect at first. It took me by surprise ... "Gerald, I don't mean to be impolite, but ... I don't think I should come visit you as much ... "

And then she was out the door. It was strange. It hurt a little. A sort of burning sensation with an occasional sharp pain when I moved, but what took me was the shock of it. The element of surprise. That dazed me more than anything. And then I started feeling numb.

8

▼

TUESDAY. 1:12 PM.

I walk out. The day is still there. I have a job. A bullshit temp job. Again. Low pay, no benefits. No shit. And eight or nine applicants waiting to take my place when I've had enough of it. And then they'll have their turn. It's sickening that I must work ... am insane, cornered, shaky ... I am disgusted by everything. Everything is philistine, common. That great intestine of the earth, industry, stinking up my breezes, taking up my time. All these people. All these little insects ... crawling and nibbling and eating away at your flesh. All these little ants and mites and fleas and ticks and mosquitoes and lice ... flying and buzzing and crawling around. Mopping and polishing and spewing their sick, worker goo all over you. All day long. Every day now. It's sickening.

9

▼

WEDNESDAY. 6:56 PM.

Ha! I have been working for the last two weeks or so. In the slave pit at Dull Computer Corporation. Lifting computer monitors up out of the crate and testing the screen colors. Averaging one paper cut per hour. Half-breeds all around. But I won't be in tomorrow, or the next day ... or the next. I'm quitting ... without notice, that is! I have procured temporary alternate income. Gratis from Libby. Yes. She has appeared ... has come through somehow! She has given me money! Amazing! Yes! I trudge along ... in and out of these meaningless little jobs. They can have their factories and their production and their numbers and their projections and they can shove it all up their greedy little asses.

Me? I'm fine ... loving it. No impending danger ... at least not for the next three or four weeks ... another vacation! Enjoy! I have become so disconnected from most things that they have started ceasing to exist. I have sunk so low in so many areas that I have actually come out the other side and am now on top somehow. I move a few inches and it's bottom ... a few inches the other way, king of the mountain again. And I don't even move myself. I let myself *be moved*. Carriage or spaceship ... reptile or human, it's all the same. You just whip out your adaptor. Life isn't made of years, only days. Days and days and more

days ... that's all there is. I have become small. Anonymous. I can slip
through cracks, ruptures, anything.

And today is a holiday. Bah! Every day is a holiday ... or a prison
term ... depending on how you look at it. We make our own rules
whether we realize it or not. It's just that the game is rigged, that's all.

We shove out our chips ... making bets here and there, some little
tiny ones, some bigger and bigger and bigger. The game goes on and
we're having a few good times along the way. A few small bets won.
Maybe a beautiful woman sitting beside you momentarily. You look at
her admiringly for a few seconds, and then back down at your cards.
The evening wears on ... new faces appear ... wander off ... your stack
grows smaller. You're winning just enough to stay in the game. But the
table feels good and the chips feel good and the velvet feels good and
you keep on playing and playing and yawn a bit and then finally it's
closing time and you look up at The Dealer and he shrugs and you lay
your four fresh aces back down on the table and walk out.

Yes. The *Pretend* Casino. This is what it is. This is what life is.
Nobody ever gets to cash in their chips. Once you finally figure this
out, you start making larger bets. Stupid bets. Silly bets. You give the
beautiful woman a playful pinch on her nice rump. And laugh at her
if she slaps you ... you tell her you're sorry and to calm down and be
sensible ... ask her for a cigarette ... her room number ... get thrown
out ... it doesn't matter. Tell the bruiser he looks like a frog ... pinch
his ass too ... he'd probably like it.

10

▼

A DAY.

I keep throwing coals into the monster. The hotbox. The engine. The engine of my century ... the engine of my condition. The only one I have. I throw for the sake of throwing. I get going fast ... whew! ... stick my head out the window ... here we are, here we are ... here we are looking for a bridge, and who cares if it's out.

Faith. This Faith wouldn't care ... she is modern somehow ... she is of her kind, but when I fly off the edge I might think of her as I careen down the side of the gorge. It will be filled with cars and faces and jobs and books. It will be filled with lasers and buttons and virtual reality. With treaties and pacts. With signings and shufflings and scramblings and adjustment. Old fears erased. New ones forming. Nations, religions running around like chickens. Capitulation. Masturbation. Adaptation. Mobilization. Plants growing out of strange places. Little wars still erupting. New confusion. New confidence. As we belch and grunt and grind and trip through the next century ... and on it'll go.

I I

▼

SATURDAY.

Have to rise early tomorrow. Yes. At least noon or so. I have another rendezvous with Libby. She is still giving me money. I am paying rent with it now. It is strange the way things develop. I met her at an old clerical job, and for the next eight or nine months she would not stop calling and would not take no for an answer. Finally I gave in. Then she began offering me "gifts."

She'd been on the off-again, on-again burner for the past year or so, like I said. The one in back. But not now. Now she's on the one in front. Yes.

I don't know what to do or say to her. And of course, she is almost twice my age. Her compliments never stop. It is baffling, and I am none of the things she says. She is still shy around me. I always have to lean over and start kissing her first. I let her tongue swim around in my mouth for one or two minutes. It is pleasant. I think of postcards … baths … how her mouth feels … my unpaid rent … now paid … trees blowing in the wind. We are, say, parked in the shade of a large department-store parking lot where I have agreed to meet her. Her hand will start wandering down my pants as I smile into her mouth. Soon we are up in my room, where she is Libby the tigress.

Most of the time it is a little hour-and-a-half-with-wine affair. A little moist afternoon nakedness between the sheets that just also happens to end with a hundred or two hundred dollars being placed in my hand before I drop her back off at her car.

It is surreal, blue-collar. Slightly intriguing. Oh, and profitable!

Later, I am alone again, thinking and smoking cigarettes. I don't mind doing it. She can have whatever she wants.

I 2

▼

A DAY.

November has come. Big and black. Cold nights of driving around, trees waving overhead down Duval Street. You arrive at a stoplight. A moment of stillness inside the car. You look around. Then the light is green and you are off again ... slowly making your way through the empty streets back to the room. Usually buzzed at some early morning hour. Everything seeming so quiet, so inoffensive. Barely any cars. Barely anything at all. Just the familiar sound of the engine and the noisy clutch and the vague notion that things will always be more or less how they are in your mind.

Seventeen hours later. Back inside. Back to looking for matches. Rummaging around. Moving books out of the way. Ignoring the phone. Glancing up at the clock. Finally it stops ringing.

I have stopped reading. There. I have stopped writing letters too. I like being left alone. I am anonymous and therefore given free rein to think and type as I please. All the windows on my train are closed. Oh, and now I can go to the ends of the earth. I get a wild hair and switch tracks ... zoom off into nowhere ... off into myself. Flirting with uncertainty, flirting with disaster. But I like it. Sometimes the train comes to a stop. I amble outside, fire up a smoke. It's cold and I don't know what time it is. A cat howls somewhere. I've been left a few times like this, but the train always comes rolling back up the tracks again sooner or later.

Once I tried to stop the train and go back to a previous stop, but it is so large ... no one can hear you. You scream, bang on the windows ... to no avail. It was then that I made up my mind to get left the next time I could. It wasn't so bad. Soon I started liking it. If you can't go back you might as well get off and mill around a while whenever you can.

I3

▼

Thursday?

Libby's purse has run dry. Yes. Shit. Actually, this is fine. I wasn't expecting it to last even this long. I will still see her occasionally. She seems to be having problems with her husband. Has to see him more. She has been naughty.

All the same, it is as if the approaching winter has a strange parallel with all the other circumstances that have filtered in through the walls to wander around in what's left of my brain. Yes. As my brain attempts to process enough thought to convey its amazement and receptivity and occasional awkwardness at the going on of the thing. The flow of the thing. Even as it turns and creeps and meanders along through the years.

Living and dying supply the fuel. Even now. All the little lives. All the little lights … floating along … little candles on the water. Each one fuel for the next. Each flame burning as if it were the first. Some lingering occasionally longer than necessary, but never dying out until the oxygen is gone. And on and on it goes … lights, river, and all toward the ocean, that great ocean of the past, where the flame will be devoured … and the river will mingle and become and disappear.

14

▼

TUESDAY. 9:00 PM.

In the end, you are always wandering around again. Back to scraping and plundering along. Walking down your strange street again. A small reel playing out. Everything is in place in spite of itself.

Yes … I was working again … at a downtown office. Shirts, ties, faxes, windows, laptops, phones. But it was either this or go under.

The office was very large. All the young girls working there almost made it bearable, but I quickly discovered how cruel and disinterested in me they all were. Still, I enjoyed the wine of their presence.

Being new, I was taken in for a while by all the sights. All the silly serious female voices. The laughter. The gossip.

For starters, and since no other space was available, I was given a supervisor's desk facing the window. It seems she was on vacation and they had nowhere else to place me. Yes. I didn't get too much work done, though. I daydreamed far too often. It was only temporary. I knew I'd be yanked any day.

I was gathering leads for one of the local computer resellers. I had just worked there myself. Down in the factory. Testing monitors. All they did was rip off the manufacturer's label and stick theirs on. A couple of months later, you sit in some office representing them to people who are probably representing somebody else to you. I figured out that it had a meaning though. It was a cog. It connected different pieces. It caused various things to continue happening somewhere down in that trite, obvious little sub-universe called business and commerce. Yes.

I quickly grew tired of it and found myself hungering for solitude. All the day long wanting to get back to my room and my typewriter and maybe some food and a phone that didn't ring. Wanting to get drunk or high or maybe nothing at all ... just sit quietly for a few hours.

I made a lot of calls to a lot of places. My favorite place to call was Georgia, for some reason. Something about the accent, naturally. My face would curve into a smile at the sound of the receptionist's voice. I would try to draw the conversation out. Maybe chat with her for just a few seconds if the proper excuse presented itself. Maybe a computer breakdown or some confusion over the spelling or pronunciation of a particularly difficult name. I was always happy when my prospect wasn't in. It gave me a few more words to say to her ... and a few more for me to hear. I always hated to actually get through to someone. That meant actually having to say something constructive. And with purpose. Something related to business. Something coming out of you like a slow, painful sigh.

What I liked everywhere, and with any accent, believe it or not, were the words "you're welcome." Not "thank you" or "good afternoon" or "hold please," but simply, "you're welcome." Something about the placement. At the end. An added little extra with a seemingly personal note. Just for you. Stretched out perfectly by a hesitation just previous.

It was over after ten or twelve days. They didn't need us anymore. There was one face in particular that I hated to leave. Lucy, the manager. She was about one-quarter Latino ... very beautiful. She was from Amarillo. Everyone loved her. I'd invented numerous questions as an excuse to walk into her office and talk to her. And there she'd sit ... slightly feline ... curled up in her chair ... feet underneath her ... shoes on the floor.

"Yes, Gerald?"

I'm sure she knew it. Always a bit of a smile at the corner of the lips. A slight fixation on the eyes. It was plenty. It was what I came in for. Those few precious glances ... her ... her hair ... her beauty mark. It was like a bit of lotion on a reddened portion of the skin. My skin, as it were, bitten and irritated to the point of a rash by the various business insects and the poison ivy of sales that thrived and bred throughout the place.

I hadn't been to The Lady in quite a while ... lack of money ... somewhat off my head ... somewhat depressed, but the sight of Lucy every day, in addition to all the other younger, bitchier, subordinate floor queens walking around, it put me under a spell for a few days again. It took all my money just to keep gas and oil in the red machine so I could sneak back and forth to work. And so for a tiny little while, Lucy was The Lady. Yes. Every morning I just wanted to throw the phone into the garbage and spend the day with Lucy ... at a park maybe ... and then to a nice cozy restaurant.

I knew I was an idiot. It's how I pass the time ... in my head mostly. It's the same everywhere.

All I had to do was get various clients to let me fax them off new product information ... that's all I was doing. Your average temp set-up ... with no benefits. I did about twenty or thirty in half as many days ... but Lucy ... she didn't seem to care. She seemed to find a certain amount of pleasure in my inadequate attempts at explanation. Actually, I was trying to explain many things, but I don't think she guessed the rest of it.

I5

▼

A DAY.

There was one more job before spring. I started working it the next week. Transung, Inc.

Yes. You know it well. Integrated circuits, electronic pagers, mobile phones, etc. The cream of the crop. A corporate fantasy. Robots, machines, schedules, production. All moving toward that great production line in the sky. Clocks … clocks everywhere. Little red neon clocks to let you know what *time* it is. As if you aren't already aware of how slow the hours crawl by as you listen to the drum and hum and whir of billions of dollars in equipment and gadgets ticking and clicking and droning away.

"We must march *onward.* We can't slack off now. It is *crucial* that we do not let up. We have *competition.*"

Unbelievable the android sub-specimens that deliver meetings … that pose as engineers, technicians, supervisors, etc. As usual, a spiritless collection of imbecility and halitosis.

I remember signing my entrance papers at the interview.

"Well, you see, the reason you are not starting off at 'experienced pay' is this new clause here that I just pulled out of my asshole. You see, I'm just one big asshole, Gerald. Just one in a larger group of many, many assholes. And we, whenever we want, can pull whatever we happen to need out of our own, or any other asshole, whenever the situation warrants it. In fact, we are so large that we can supply enough shit to last all of you your entire lifetime. Amazing, isn't it. And beautiful in a way ... wouldn't you say so?"

It comes out of their buttoned-down little eyes as you're sitting in some office. Some dull cell of an office, with drawers and shelves everywhere. And always a picture or two ... a couple of their brats smiling at the ball game ... and little sheets of paper up on the walls ... little emblems, little graphs, done up in glass ... all sorts of ingenious devices to keep track of chips! ... and *labor*! ... and *profits*!

Yes. I drive in every afternoon now. Down Research Boulevard. A sickening stretch of parking lots, strip malls, red lights, and gas stations.

I walk in. I've done this many times before. I trudge down the long hall every day to the Hell that waits at the soon-approaching hour of three. Slipping down, down, down the stairs to the giant underground whir of machines and little blue space suits and the roving eyes of the supervisors.

16

▼

A DAY.

Am insane with thoughts of quitting … am gasping with it.

I am sliding through these pages … in my head and elsewhere. I have no thought but spillover.

But yes, a new one. Out of nowhere. Natasha. A stripper. Lovely ass. Friendly. Intelligent. Young. A fleshy surprise. Knocking on my little door. A Saturday. Late in the evening. A perfect one-nighter.

I had spied her the previous weekend … writhing … squirming in a tight red dress at Exposé. A mere phone call, and a week later she is sitting on my couch … looking around … perusing books. Her warmth fills the room. She asks questions, we smoke … talk softly. She is young, polite, sexual.

I am sitting opposite her, at my table, five or six feet away. Slowly she slides off the couch as I am speaking and crawls over to the chair in front of me and curls herself around on her knees and sits down and puts her arms in my lap and begins to play with my hands.

I look down at her … my thoughts trail off. She opens my palm up and slowly strokes it with the ends of her fingers. My mouth tilts slightly open. I forget what I am saying. She runs her fingers up the length of my arm, brushing it gently with her fingernails. I reach into her hair.

She begins to speak, all the while stroking my palm and my arms.

"Do you read a lot?"

"Sometimes."

A few moments pass.

"Your arms are thin ... but strong ... almost graceful."

"Thank you."

"I like the way you talked in the club. I hate everyone there."

All the while I am looking down at her ... this marvelous little creature, this strange beautiful specimen, lending her magical female form and presence. After you have starved for a while, it doesn't even seem real, even if it's right in front of you again. You keep touching it, waiting for it to disappear. Eventually it does anyway.

But for a while it is there. Unbelievable, but it is there. Right in front of you ... a sort of eternity ... with legs. And you remember loneliness, but suddenly your mouth is on a neck. A soft, beautiful neck and the moment is young and perfect and you run with it.

17

X.

My luck has run out. They found me at last. Yes. I was arrested yesterday morning. Tuesday. It seems that records of my various vehicular infractions were beginning to show up downtown.

Yes. Seven o'clock in the morning … a knock on the door … my little castle invaded by fascists! Hello, how are you!?! Suddenly, I am given a brief explanation of what is about to happen and then given a few moments to dress and then I am handcuffed and led out to the squad car and driven off to jail to be booked.

We arrive at the jail and they lead me past the drunk tank to a room with various guards and forms and questions.

"Do you feel suicidal … ?"

"Yes."

"Yes?"

"I mean no … "

"No? … "

"No."

"Do you have a history of mental illness?"

"No."

"Do you have any medical conditions that we should be aware of?"

"No."

"Do you have any drugs hidden on you?"

"No."

"Do you have an attorney?"

"No."

"Do you have a job?"

"Yes."

"Where?"

"Transung, Inc."

"What do you do there?"

"Manufacturing."

"How long have you been employed there?"

"Six weeks."

"How long have you lived in Austin?"

"Six years in the city limits. Ten years in the immediate area. I was born in Houston."

"Step into this room."

I step into a side room with four or five others. A guard appears.

"Please remove all of your clothing."

We remove all of our clothing. He walks around inspecting us to make sure we don't have any weapons hidden. We are then given gray jumpsuits and led off down a corridor to our cell block.

We walk down to C2. The cells are little, seven-by-eight-foot squares of iron and concrete, with two single beds hanging down from a chain on the side of the wall and a dirty stainless-steel commode over on the left, flanked by what used to be a shower.

The lower bunk is occupied. Someone appears to be asleep under a blanket. I walk in.

The door slams behind me, and I clamber up onto the top bunk and try to get comfortable. I look around. There is a tiny barred rectangular window in the middle of the door down to my left. Besides that, not much. The rectangle is the only thing in the immediate area that is open.

There I sit for about eleven or twelve hours. The monotony is interrupted twice, by a sandwich and some flavored water being delivered through the window for us and a phone-call break that I decline to use.

You sit there. Occasionally there is hollering and singing from a transient in another cell. Nobody speaks that much really. You continue sitting there. Everything runs in front of your eyes. Your life. You picture it ending there. Never being allowed to leave because of some mistake in the paperwork. A week. Two weeks. A month. A year ... ten years.

The hours pass on. Eventually, after what seems like an eternity, my name is called by a guard and the door opens and I am led out of the block and down a hall where I am handcuffed in single file with twenty or thirty others from various sections of the jail and marched into a large courtroom for a late evening session. We sit on benches in the courtroom all handcuffed to each other. Presently the judge enters and we rise. He goes over the charges and asks us how we are going to plead and then gives each of us a sentence.

And then after the court session I am finally freed, walking back home finally ... 7:30 PM, released out a side door at Seventh Street and Red River, sentenced to 140 hours of community service.

I am home again now.

I am just beginning to think of how offensive this is.

I don't feel like writing now. I am trying to think of how to get out of it. It seems impossible. It is impossible.

I have no ambitions or desires anymore. I just go with it now ... am continually looking off at nothing. I get sick, laugh ... fall into despair ... think of philosophy, history, pistols, pills, World War III, IV.

I imagine my death will be something like running out of gas finally on an open stretch of highway ... and that will be that ... it seems so silly.

Thus I draw my little pictures. I experiment out of boredom. I laugh at them. I love them. I don't know what else to do.

18

▼

Saturday. 8:00 am.

I report to Zilker Park for the first eight of my 140 hours of community service. I park, walk to a sort of metal barn up the hill from Barton Springs, just in back of the playground and the swings and the trains and the outdoor theatre.

Holy shit! A motley collection of Neanderthals, adolescents, drunks, and various minor drug off enders. The supervisor stands there calling out names ... making sure we're all there. His name is Frank. We stand around for a few minutes.

"Bryan Elsworth?"

"Present."

"Roland Martinez?"

"Present."

"Gerald Mitkof?"

"Present."

I try not to feel depressed. It's almost interesting in a certain shitty kind of way. Eventually we are broken up into groups and sent off with our little sub-supervisors with their little Parks and Recreation Department uniforms. Mostly Latino, with a couple whites and a single black.

I am put on trash duty. Naturally. Three of us pile into a truck and we speed off to the nether regions of the park with our trash bags and our sulks and our sleepy discontent. There we are dispatched to our little sectors and our trash cans with a few brief instructions on where to rendezvous at a certain time.

I walk off toward the first trash can. It is absurd. The whole thing. I stand there for a second looking at it, and then back up and around at the cursed white truck cruising slowly around the park. Sometimes you wonder how you get to certain points in your life. Then you don't wonder anymore.

I look back down at the trash can, put on my gloves. It is overflowing. Bags and bottles and banana peelings and diapers and cans. I spread out my trash bag and start picking everything up off the grass and putting it in there. Then I fashion the bag over the top of the can and turn it over on its side and then back over into the bag again.

The first one is done. I look up at the sky and then amble off toward the next can with my huge bag trailing behind me.

I suddenly think of Santa Claus. Yes. Go Prancer … and Blitzen … go Rancid … and Vixen. And something for little Johnny … and little Mary … and little Susie … and little Tommy … and little Jimmy. Ho ho ho! And to all a good night! Meeerrrrry Christmas!

I finish my first round and deposit three huge bags of trash into the waiting white truck, where I then collect more bags and wander off toward the toilets and the picnic tables. The truck drives off. I take my bags and walk in between the outdoor pissers. I stand there for a second … look around. It is about 10:30 AM by this time. I position myself so that I am hidden between the trees and the toilets but still have a commanding view of the road for when the bastard white Parks and Recreation truck comes driving up again. I look over to my right. One of my compatriots takes my cue, drops his bags, hides himself. He is about sixty yards off. Our gaze meets. I give him a jerk of the head.

I take my gloves off, pull out a cigarette, light it, inhale deeply. The wind blows just a bit. Out on the field a woman is playing with her dog. I look off at her. The dog is large and brown, with soft fur and a big, happy, dumb dog face. She throws a stick about eighty feet out into the grass, and the dog fetches it and then runs back to her. They do this several times. I stand there watching them, hidden between the two toilet rooms. Finally the dog jumps up on her and she laughs and he barks and they collapse on the grass and roll all over one another and the dog is barking his fool head off and he begins to get a little excited and starts pawing at her and nudging and rooting his head all in her armpits and crotch and barking and biting her legs and stomach and shoulders. She is laughing and it goes on for a while and finally she wrestles him off of her and staggers up as he runs circles around her, growling and barking and suddenly he takes off running at breakneck speed, sprinting clear across the field, and I lean my head out to watch him and it is a little brown blur advancing quickly through the green and he runs out of sight as she walks slowly in his direction calling out his name. In a few seconds he comes panting back up to her, and they disappear down a long sloping hill.

I look back up toward the road just in time to catch the top of the truck cruising slowly toward us. I put out my cigarette, drift on. The truck jumps the curb, heads over to me. I pick up a few pieces of scattered trash out on the field, move toward the truck. It pulls up. The window goes down. It is Saul, the black. He's about thirty-five. I get ready for a rebuke. A heavy low voice comes out of the truck.

"Say, little man, check it out. Frank's in his office doin' some paper work. Iz break time and I'm goin' to the store for a cold one, so why don'tcha just get lost for an hour or so and I'll be back to pick ya up by the construction signs. Now listen. You see Frank pullin' up you look busy, you got it? He'll be driving the big truck … the one wit the logo on the side … ya got it?"

I wink at him. "I got it."

He pulls off. I move on up the hill. My companions are lost as well. I wander around for a while and eventually find a picnic table in a somewhat secluded section of trees. It overlooks a large expanse of field south of Barton Springs Road. From there I can see all the roads and pathways leading up to the area.

I sit there, smoking cigarettes, look down at my trash bag … eventually start wondering where everybody else is. It is a game here … like anything else.

I look up at the city. All the banks and high-rises and office buildings. All the cars and ants and movement snaking up and around through all the grid and hum and asphalt and green and glass of the city. Puffing and crawling and motoring along. And the powerhouse southwest of the city … like a big electric gland. Bristling and popping and glowing with an odd network of structures and angularities and laws and lines.

And then the Parks and Recreation Department. A support mechanism. But with a few bolts loose and vibrating somehow. As always. It seems silly and bureaucratic. But necessary. I stamp out my cigarette ... wander off toward the hiking trails.

19

▼

SUNDAY.

I am down to ninety-six hours. I keep them marked off on my little yellow strip of paper. These little marks. They mean a lot. They represent something.

Frank is on vacation. All the other little sub-supervisors take it easy. Make jokes about him, his wife ... the cut of his pants.

We break up into our little groups. First we are to clean up the play area. There has been a birthday party or something of the like out by the picnic tables and the train. Two or three of us make the rounds, picking up little party gags and wrapping paper and bows and ribbon and paper plates and cups and soda wrappers and leftovers and putting them away, and then off several rounds on the truck and out to the dumpster. We have to hurry because another group has reserved the area for some similar function in another hour or two.

I walk over to the cans, dumping them over into my bag. I approach can number three, knock it over on its side. Suddenly an army of wasps come pouring out in squadrons of four, six, and eight. They quickly pick me up and come zeroing in on my head and arms and shoulders as I curse and back off. Suddenly it's a war! Out of nowhere!

I give ground ... swatting and flailing mightily with my hand full of empty bags. They won't let up. Circling and diving in, and I am pawing and fighting and backing up, and I manage to backhand a few of them senseless with my free hand and my peers have stepped back to view the spectacle. They keep coming ... wave after wave pouring out from the trash can ... zeroing in on the great human monster that has interrupted their feast ... and it is a magnificent battle and I am exhilarated and valiant ... yes ... a young Greek hero! ... armed with his trash bags! A battle of land creatures! They don't want our young hero to enter the coveted Cave of Virgins! They've sent their tiny flying demons! Yes. But they will not stop me!

I keep backing up. Absurdity! I knock them off into space, but half of them keep circling back in, and they've launched the whole unit ... they've emptied the barracks ... for every one I cripple, two more buzz in to take his place.

Eventually, they back me clear off the playground as the supervisor stands there laughing and telling me to be more careful next time.

I walk off to the utility shed. I know where a little something is that will tickle their tummies. I enter, start digging around in back where all the supplies are. Then I spot it, give a slow little snicker. I reach down into the box, pull out two cans of industrial-sized insecticide. Yes ...

I walk back out toward the picnic tables, approach the trash warily. It's scattered everywhere. I peer up inside the cave from six or eight feet off. They have resumed their feast. Reyes (the shift supervisor, of sorts) calls out in his little Mexican voice, "Be caaareful. Yu know wha happen las time." He chuckles.

Three or four of them tried to escape. They didn't make it ...

Reyes is so amused and delighted at this that after lunch, he puts two of us on "canoe duty." Yes. This was to become for me the greatest time waster and screw-off method ever discovered in the whole history of United States Community Service. I eventually used this method to waste whole afternoons and evenings at a time.

But at first it was just a game. Something given as a reward for some bit of entertainment provided.

Yes ... at about 1:20 PM Reyes, myself, and a young punk-ass redhead named Vick are trotting down the hill to the tributary that feeds Town Lake where it widens out just south of the 1st Street bridge.

Vick's about sixteen. Short buzzed red hair. Fair skin. Freckles. Wiseass. He's out here for some curfew violation at his high school. Has twenty-four hours.

Reyes is barking instructions.

"Now listen. Don't fall over and drown ... okay. You ever been in a canoe before? Okay, now when you get out into the lake, I want you to work the edges and shorelines and pick up all the trash that is hung in and around the trees and branches. But first, I want you to follow me down the creek a ways. There's a trash can that's in the water a couple of feet down that I want you to get."

We walk down to the bank, to all the canoes and the shed and the Sunday customers. We select a vessel and two paddles and begin placing it into the edge of the water.

"Now here ... take some life jackets ... and don't be stupid, okay ... now just follow me up here a little ways."

He walks off.

Vick makes his way gently to the back of the canoe, and I shove off and crawl over the bow and get myself situated. The canoe is a slender, silver, two-man affair ... roughly twelve feet long with little black numbers stamped on the stern and bow.

We begin gliding slowly across the water, paddling smoothly along, and we make our way up underneath a bridge as Reyes descends down a steep embankment to meet us at the water's edge.

"You see it? It's right down there. That big blue-looking thing."

Vick suddenly pipes up.

"Wait, I want to get it."

And so ... maneuvering the canoe around so the young Vick can prove his manhood. Paddling sideways and then forward and moving his end of the canoe up to this submerged plastic hunk resting underwater just off the bank.

"Wait. Wait. I've got to get closer. I can't reach it."

Now Reyes barking again.

"Yeah. That's it. That's it. Shit ... Don't fall in ... use your paddle ... use your paddle. Here, see if you can move it over to me. Yeah. Yeah. Can you move it?"

I keep placing Vick over the top of the trash can. We drift back just a ways, and then I maneuver him up again and attempt to keep him right above it, paddling and switching sides and looping little figure eights in the water with my paddle.

Vick again.

"I can't get my hand under it."

"Shit."

We drift back once more. The canoe turns completely around in the breeze and the slight current.

Meanwhile, a chorus of ducks has coasted up to inspect the goings on. They meander in and around the brush and the arches to jabber and babble and gawk … with their bobbing necks and their blank, questioning little eyes.

Reyes looks off, then back down at the water. We are underneath the Barton Springs Road Bridge. It is a lovely day. A silly strange afternoon. In the corner of the city. A city among cities.

Once again I move Vick up into position, where I then lean to one side of the canoe so he can reach down far enough into the water to get his hand on the elusive trash can.

Reyes again.

"You got it. You got it. Can you lift it?"

And finally, after much absurdity and effort and wetness, the young Vick manages to lift the damn thing up into the canoe as I lean and balance and struggle to keep us from going overboard and into the water. Success at last.

And then a few minutes later, we are sailing back upstream to the landing with our trophy (the trash can) perched in the middle between us with the ducks following curiously behind. A little water parade parting the creek.

We transfer it to Reyes, and soon we are moving back down the creek toward Town Lake. Yes. Vick and I, a strange pair … strong-arming it down the middle of the stream. We both light up cigarettes. Vick pulls a hat out of his pocket. I turn around. Take it all in. The green shoreline and the trees and bushes in the background … the ducks crossing our wake lazily, twenty or thirty feet back … off to other interests … Vick rowing gallantly … cigarette hanging out of his mouth … smoke curling out on both sides of his head and disappearing behind his head … the sun glinting off the water behind him.

I had to hold it there for a few seconds. Take it in some more. The whole scene. The whole afternoon. Sometimes a ray of circumstance parts the misery just long enough for you to see again.

I turn back around, resume paddling. The turtles move out of the way, and we slice their rings now … moving on … past bridges and mishaps … past debris and deterrent.

And soon out in the lake, coming to rest slowly … held up magically by the surface of the water. And to the north, the city … half a mile off … maybe more … taking up half the view, and the railroad bridge idly filling up the expanse … stretching somehow all the way to the other side. And back around to the lake … such an odd green pocket of wetness. All the structure and iron and liquid laying all around you.

We are perched on the surface, and soon the young Vick reaches into his pocket and pulls out a mangled joint, which we proceed to smoke carefully and nervously.

And there we waste the remainder of the afternoon. Paddling up and down at our fancy. Drifting along. Buzzed and alert and dreamy and alive. Wasting time. Idly picking up stray pieces of trash to put in our bags. Hours begin to pass.

And then late in the evening again, the day wasted, rowing back up under the railroad bridge to catch a passing train. We center ourselves directly underneath the main section. It is shaded and huge. About thirty feet above us. A crisscrossing of metal and rust and lines and wood and arches and cement pillars, with all this vibration and rattle and pop and clatter right up above you. We sit there looking up at it. Sitting there directly underneath it. High. This idiotic iron beast. Clacking and leaning and squeaking with much effort and force and noise, all the while a droning symmetry of wheel and track being driven over in the background.

It rolls past. The sound disappears down the track. We sit there. A minute. Five minutes. We're both stunned. Speechless at the effect.

Suddenly we realize it is late. Very late. We begin rowing back and making our way back down the lake and finally turning in to the tributary … rowing tiredly and firm now … back through the turtles and the algae … moving quickly … back under the Barton Springs Bridge and finally all the way up to the launch.

It is deserted. No one around except a few walkers. We are paranoid, slightly nervous. We get out and pull the canoe up and place it with the others and store the oars in their box and walk up to the barn, only to find it empty and locked and the parking lot absent of cars.

We depart after a brief deliberation on our state of affairs, ending in a confident dismissal of any knowledge of wrongdoing, complete with accompanying alibi.

I walk to my car, open the door, get in, and start the engine. My clock reads 5:48 PM.

I drive in.

20

▼

THURSDAY. 1:35 AM.

I hardly write anymore. Night passes into day, and I care or think nothing of it.

Soon I will be stepping off into wilderness and madness and open air. I've decided to head north. Way north: Alaska.

Yes. I have little peanut-sized worries, but they will soon fall off my nimble shoulders. My debt of community service will have been paid, and I will be free to walk off into never.

My lovely bed that I cannot depart from will be kept in a storage facility, and my sportster will relax in a driveway. I have managed to save $1,000, with which I have just purchased a plane ticket to Seattle and a three-day ferry pass to Petersburg, where I will look for work on a salmon vessel or, failing that, a cannery. This should be interesting. I shall explore and expose the Alaskan myth. I've been hearing so much about it lately that I cannot resist. It is an absurd logic that guides such things.

You see, I just water the garden. I have my subtle flowers to look out for. You never plant what grows there. It just sprouts up. It has been planted there sometime when you were away, and then it develops a certain charm after a while.

You find what finds you. Usually it's a mood. Or an urge. Or a woman. But there it is. There it is, and then there you go.

21

▼

SATURDAY.

Repairing a broken ditch at Barton Springs. Standing around with one or two minor convicts. We are carrying little buckets of water from the creek to be mixed with the concrete. I stand there watching Reyes apply the mixture. Suddenly he babbles something in Spanish to Felix, another sub-supervisor.

"Hey ... what's your name ... "

Felix attempts to address me.

"Wrap up all this hose lying around here ... and when you get finished with that, take the wheelbarrow and go up to the barn and get some more concrete and bring it out here ... "

I bring the concrete. We wait around, go to lunch, come back. More of the same. We disappear for an hour or two to make a few trash rounds. The day passes.

22

▼

SUNDAY.

The afternoon young. I passed the morning cleaning bathrooms, raking mulch and leaves, and then picking dead branches from the rosebushes across the street by the arboretum ... minus one glove. Once I pricked myself. A tiny drop of red appeared on my finger. It seemed like a cliché. I licked the blood. Stood there looking at it.

So strange to perform these little duties for the city.

And later, out in the canoe. Alone. Just me this time.

I paddle out into the lake. Everything surreal and silent, with that odd watery motion wallowing all beneath you. I glide dreamily along the banks. Daydream. Move my paddle with a sort of lazy precision. I watch the swirls. Switch sides. Drift. I am clueless and buzzed. The water is slightly fascinating. I tap it playfully and flat. It seems so obvious. All those handfuls and cupfuls. Filling up itself. Sitting there in the earth. Some strange shade of green.

Next, a tiny island. Held together by a railway arch. There is a small scattering of brush and plants. I move toward it ... moor my little vessel ... walk up to the largest root ... look around for snakes and reptiles ... find none ... sit down to smoke.

There I stay for maybe an hour or so. Looking around ... smoking ... playing with leaves and little pieces of stick.

Eventually, I decide to row up to the Sheraton Hotel that overlooks the lake on the south side. I think a couple of drinks are in order! Yes, yes, Splendid!

I push off, start paddling ... make it ... two or three hundred yards, gazing about, slightly nervous, snickering to myself.

I drift up into the grass next to the sailboat launch, maneuver myself onto the shore, and pull my tiny craft up onto the lawn a bit. I stand there looking around. A few cars. A few walkers. Everything calm and inoffensive. I survey the scene for a few more seconds and then begin the satisfied, lazy stroll up into the lobby and down the hall to the bar, where I order a vodka and orange juice. I walk over to a large leather chair, get comfortable, sit my drink down on the end table, glance around the room. The bartender is polite, virtually unseen. It's the middle of the day.

I sit there sipping my drink. Finish. Get up and walk to the bar. Order another. Sit down again. It is pleasant. I go find a newspaper and sit down again. Start flipping through it. The front page, the world news, the local briefs, the entertainment section, the life section, the movie reviews, the book reviews, the editorials, the classified section. Reading leisurely, detached, thoughtless. Sitting there, flipping pages. The paper rustling occasionally.

A half-hour passes. Maybe more. Suddenly, four middle-aged business types descend from the stairs and transport their bodies up to the bar. I sniff, look back down at my paper. I look off, pick my drink up. Naturally, sounds begin coming from their frontal orifices. Unpleasant, odious sounds. Sounds like by-products or waste or fatty tissue. Like large wafts of diarrhea rolling off their tongues. First one and then the other. And then occasionally all at the same time. And then rising in pitch and volume and stench with the movements of the jaw. A sort of blabbering chorus of toiletries and commodes flushing. A symphony of turds drifting out into the air.

Eventually, the room begins to stink.

I make my way outside and back down onto the grass that rolls down toward the lake. I sit down on a bench, smoke, look at my little canoe down there by the water. I think vaguely of my duties, my superiors.

23

▼

MONDAY. 12:25 AM.

It is over. It is all over.

I return to this room each night ... am greeted by wine bottles and gentle bohemian smell ... by ash and wax and dusty forgiveness.

My head is reeling from last days of work and wine and leaf.

I've fallen through. I'm free-falling into waste and magic and open sky. Everything is odd and threadbare.

Heron with Saturday's shit on its toes. Life going down its gullet like a young mackerel. Yesterday Kian and I ... drinking wine and gesticulating on a floating deck. A merry little band farting gentle melodies to the children. They sit around in a circle like young enchanted mice.

We sit in the sky and yawn sleepily at the sun. We beckon the days. Life ceases to be different from anything we've ever known.

PART 3

▼

I

▼

MAY.

We are scheduled to pull out from the port of Bellingham, just north of Seattle. Yes. It's an old, white, slow-moving ship. The Alaska Marine Highway's finest. *The Columbia.*

I am deck class. With all the other extras and alsos and workers. It's perfect. What deck class means is that you didn't purchase an actual room but will pitch a tent and sleep out on Deck 2, stern side.

We get off the bus from the airport and eventually make our way inside a large silver building. And then another. And another. I walk slowly through them with my luggage on my back. It takes several minutes. They all look like airplane hangars. I find my way down a hall and to the main ticket window, where I stand in line waiting to get my paperwork stamped. Next, a series of corridors and roped-off areas, and finally up a plank to the ship, where I get out my ticket and show it to the attendant. Then I board and walk around and amble around the halls and corridors and decks for a bit. Eventually I find a little spot at the stern of the ship up against a back deck wall, where I proceed to erect my little plastic home and begin the journey.

Setting it up takes about fifteen or twenty minutes. I stand there reading my directions and piecing together all these little rods and flaps and snaps. Pulling all this fabric down over everything. Finally I work it into shape. I stretch it out, anchor everything down. I throw in my luggage bag and check all my tickets and crawl inside and zip down the window and sit back and get comfortable.

I sit there. Looking out this little flap. Sitting inside this little mushroom on the back deck of the ship. With all the other nobodies and travelers.

I look around. All this scrambling around for room, all this gear being tossed about everywhere, all these belongings and voices and bodies and lines of people running back and forth over the planks. All these ropes. All these little men in buttoned-down blue shirts and ties and jackets with little pins on their shoulders walking around with clipboards and papers.

Finally, everyone seems to be on board. The plank is shoved back into the side of the ship as everyone continues to mill around and converse and get comfortable. Everybody has their own deck where they have to sleep, but until then you're free to roam the ship.

Soon the horn sounds, and it has begun. We disengage, begin to drift slowly away from the dock and out into the cold green waters of Bellingham Bay just north of Puget Sound.

Suddenly everything is windy, alive. Slightly exhilarating. The dock starts to drift slowly away from us. The minutes begin to pass.

We slowly make our way out toward the Straits of Georgia. Everyone milling around, talking. A strange load of youth and foreigners and vacationing elderly.

An hour passes. On we go. Through the strait now. We begin to make for the open sea, moving farther and farther north. Soon we are cutting through wind and whales and choppy seas and a few miles off are the heavy green woods of Vancouver and British Columbia. Our destination is the Inside Passage. Petersburg, Alaska.

Out back there is a bit of excitement and anxiety. We know what we're in for. Everyone in deck class. We try to pretend it's not waiting for us in Alaska. The hunt for work and food and money. Yes, for now we're just vacationing … like the old geezers. A Sunday cruise. Yes. Have some tea! Stretch out a bit!

The hair blowing. I'm feeling slightly giddy. Smoking a cigarette over the railing. Laughing a bit at nothing. Looking down again at the water. Imagining falling in. Looking down, down, down over the side at all the green fairy-tale water. And then back up, two, three, four hundred yards off. All the endless acres of waves rolling out all around you. Everything cresting and swelling in motion. The wind blowing. The ship carving a white, scraggly "V" slowly across the surface. And then imagining if it sunk. Imagining wetness and absurdity and cold. Looking around at all the people and the potential mayhem.

And later roaming all over the ship. Down into the bowels and hallways and bathrooms. All the little cabins ... all the little handles and numbers. All the doors and drawings and measurements and capacities pinned up all over the walls. All the little pictures and dimensions.

It seems this particular vessel first set sail in 1972. Hmmm. Looking up at all the various routes taken by all the ships since the beginning.

Yes. Walking off finally and then up a flight of stairs where I decide to check on seating possibilities in the restaurant. The nice one. I chat up my companions, other workers traveling up. We check out the menus. Put our names on the list. Then I amble back out on top again. The sun begins to set. The ship moves on.

And then later on that evening after dinner. (I had the shrimp, rice, and chowder.) Coming back out from a drink in the bar. Floating up the steps late at night and out the door to the railing. Feeling invigorated. Windy. Sea-buzzed. Everybody's half drunk. (I had just blown twenty-four dollars.)

I turn around, bid my companions good evening, amble up next to the cold white iron white wall, light up a cigarette. I start to walk back off toward the bow. I exhale largely and satisfactorily, the hair blowing around the face a bit. I watch my little cloud of smoke drifting along down the side of the railing. For a second it's still moving. It still has the ship. And then it glides quickly out over the side, out over the sea. Suspended. Thirty feet in the air. Drifting finally out into nothing.

Yes, so very strange ... having one more cigarette and then back down to the stern and groping and stumbling around to your little plastic round room. Amid other assorted shapes and varieties of exposed, plastic round rooms. A little field of blue mushrooms all growing out back in the middle of the night. And then finding your own little blue mushroom with its special markings and unzipping your little mushroom door and then inside and zipping it most of the way back up. And then taking off your clothes, everything cold and slightly moist. Then slithering inside your dry little cocoon, and you can hear the wind blowing outside, and beneath you is the feel and hum and drone and dreamy subdued power of the engines carrying you along. A gray metal ghost moving slowly over the water. Nothing around it but the night.

And momentarily your body heat fills your little cocoon and you begin to get warm and eventually your lovely, slight drunkenness begins to hit you and suddenly you feel secure and cozy and pacified.

You lie there. Glowing. Perched out on the back deck in the middle of the night. Perched on this little ship. This little speck of lights and life. Sailing away under the stars. Sailing away on the black nothing of the ocean. You feel serene and silly and laugh out loud for a second. A little outburst. A little chirp of ecstasy.

Then you can't remember anything else.

It went on for three days.

2

▼

WEDNESDAY.

We docked at Petersburg. A fishing village situated on a tiny island just off the Canadian coast. It's maybe three or four miles long. Mostly forests and mountains.

It is my third day here. I'm writing this from inside my tent at Swamp Shitty, the campground outside of town where they herd the riffraff of the island. It's where I've ended up. The only place I could find once I got off the ship. Picture it, yes? A rainforest at the base of the mountains just in back of the city. Yes. A veritable swamp with a network of walkways leading out to an uncertain scattering of wooden platforms, sixteen or seventeen in all, upon one of which I have pitched my mini round mushroom home, where I will be spending the next number of unknown weeks.

*   *   *   *

The first thing I've noticed are the birds. They start up at about four-thirty in the morning right at sunrise. Every morning. Very large blackbirds. Murderous, screeching things. They descend down from the rainforest to inspect the grounds and laugh at us.

It's all struggle and escape. The birds know it.

I'm going out for a walk.

Welcome to Alaska.

3

▼

SATURDAY.

I am high now and somewhat content. I'm sitting here inside my tent. The wind outside seems natural enough. Just there, somehow. Inhuman. Beautiful. A cool, mindless roar rolling down out of the summer hills.

There is a slight apprehension and exhilaration to the days here. Every afternoon I've been getting up and walking into town to the docks and accosting boat captains. All to no avail. They've already hired someone or they're still doing this or that or something or other. Ah, but the boat captains. Beastly specimens, some of them. One or two are congenial and somewhat pleasant, but the lot of them are possessed. Yes. With their mechanical little contraptions and their wrinkles and their dark faces and their suspenders. With their boots and their stares and their shotguns and their maps and their radios and their antennas and their horns and their strange little names on their little vessels.

What? This one here? He hates mainlanders? Good. I'll stop by tomorrow.

More than likely it's off to Ocean Queen for me. The salmon cannery. A dull, tomb-like thing down a dock out over the water. A cold green dungeon on stilts. I figured it would come to this.

But for now, I am playing inside my little blue heaven. My cold little nirvana. Filled with marijuana. Filled with cigarettes and icy grin. I bounce off the walls. My face comes out of my boots. Orion 3. The glacier belt. Dreaming betazoids and bliss. Dreaming sky wine and smooth sectors.

4

▼

SUNDAY.

I wake up inside my blue little womb. It's roughly the length of my body. I lay there. In a sort of suspension. Drifting in and out of sleep.

The images roll over my eyes. So much already. The hunt for work. Trips to the restroom facility up the hill, out the main walkway. Ice-cold water for your face and neck. Hours and hours of walks through the rainforest down from the campground. The beach. Various excursions through Petersburg. A leftover Norwegian settlement, come alive for the summer. And then more conversations with cannery managers, fishermen. Long spells spent sitting on benches down by the docks, taking in the boats, the mountains across the water on the mainland. Smoking. Watching the eagles.

I open my eyes again eventually, look up at the top of my tent. It is a tiny sphere of blue above my head. It looks like a skyline.

My head is poking out the end of my brown little quilt. I look around ... blink ... reach my hand out and touch the color ... scratch it gently ... push it a little ... yes ... it is there ... and I am here inside. I am definitely here inside ... this much I know. Everything seems quiet still, except for a slight wind.

Several minutes seem to pass. I continue to stare upward. Another minute. Another. The shapes begin to blend and blur slightly. I seem to drift. Reality slips a bit.

I float along in my plastic bubble. It seems natural. I drift and drift. How odd! How odd to be drifting along in this blue little nest of sky. Sometimes it's all the sky you need.

I slip into sleep for several minutes.

Presently the wind blows outside. I come to.

The sensation recalls the warm days of childhood, when you get up from an afternoon nap and can't remember what day it is or where you're at for a second.

I can hear noises. Somebody is grilling freshly caught fish in the campground. I can hear birds screeching.

The blackbirds are always fighting the eagles for the scraps. Everybody loves it. The eagles have a good go at them.

The eagles usually win.

5

▼

TUESDAY AFTERNOON.

I'm still at the campground. Have just started working. It was Wednesday I think. Or Thursday. I walk a mile or so down to the docks every day now at 8:00 AM for my sixteen hours. Down the runway and into the cannery. It is a collection of five or six green tin buildings. Really nasty.

First of all, we were given a brief meeting about the hazards of the job and the long hours and the working conditions. Then sent upstairs to collect our rain gear and our gloves and boots.

The first two shifts, there weren't many salmon. The runs hadn't started coming in yet. We spent a few hours cleaning the machines and wiping down the belts before being sent away for the day.

And then on Saturday afternoon, the supervisor gathers us all up and lines everybody up and gives us brief instructions on handling and sharpening our scrapers and knives as well as various methods of cutting as we stand beside a large trough with a stream of cold water running down through it. There are eight or ten people on each side. Mostly foreigners.

There are several different troughs in several different rooms, depending upon what type of cut or preparation is being performed.

Out at the end of the main corridor is a large winch and a collection of pulleys and cables that transport the fish from the boats up into the main hold. From there, the fish are directed to their respective areas and operations.

In a half-hour or so they started coming. Mostly kings and reds. Huge things. Unbelievable! Two and three and four feet long. Sliding and tumbling and careening down the trough. Hundreds ... thousands. All silver and white and red and pink and black. It was almost beautiful at first. All these sea creatures with their graceful streamlined bodies and their cold black eyes and their icy strange lives. So robust and healthy. So singular and simple. Raw with sex and hunger and instinct. Nothing else. The art of the Earth.

You stand there looking at them. Slightly amazed. The first five or six fish you can't cut right and they come away rather mangled and unattractive and the supervisor is there scolding you for playing and staring at them.

Soon I get the hang of it. Quickly I am exhausted and become dazed and mechanical and unthinking, with as little output as possible. The fish aren't pretty anymore. The minutes and hours start to pass. The machines drone on. You switch legs ... switch arms ... switch knives. They keep coming. We all try to keep up as best we can, but there is a constant clog up at the end of the trough and occasionally the fish spill out onto the floor and there is hollering and jabbering and clambering around as we struggle to lift the bastards back into the trough.

This keeps going on and on, and finally somehow we break at noon for the first lunch. This entails piling into a bus and driving a third of a mile down to the kitchen, where we stand in line with our plates and our fatigue and our tired, hungry silence. The kitchen is a small, dilapidated cafeteria. The food is decent enough, though. Baked salmon. Imagine. With whipped potatoes and salad. And every once in a while some pasta and sauce with bread. There are some desserts as well. All manner of beverages.

But the way the bus schedule runs, you only get about eighteen to twenty minutes to actually sit down and eat your meal. Thus, it is consumed very quickly and methodically in large bites with little thought. The rest of the hour is spent climbing in and out of your rain gear and riding or waiting on the bus. Then there is a quick break outside for a smoke before climbing back on and driving away to the cannery again.

A few hours pass. At five or so we lunch for the second time and then it's back to work.

You walk back in again. Down the main corridor and into a small room to dig out your rain gear. It is wet and cold. Your face sours slightly as you put it back on. There are other bodies moving around. Ugly, strange things, usually to be avoided. And then out the door and around the corner and back up to the line where you wait for the signal to be given to start the machines. In a few minutes, everything starts running again. The first fish you grab doesn't seem real. Your arms are slightly refreshed but still tired. After about thirty minutes, your perception of time is so altered that it could be six-thirty or it could be eight or nine for all you know. The only sounds are the machines running and the cans scudding down behind us and the occasional hollering or shouting if something has gone wrong.

On it goes. On and on. All these creatures and all this energy and machinery. You look around. A strange hell. Twenty or thirty specimens ... all looking down ... all in bright yellow rain gear. Their hoods down over their faces. Serious, ugly faces. Faces of exhaustion. Faces of amphetamines. Mechanical faces with stone jaws and cold lips and ugly eyes and two long arms making repetitive, strange, jerky movements over and over. And the blade working its banal, sure magic. All this iron and flesh and tissue and mechanization. Like a system. Like a single thought. Rattling and grinding and pumping and cutting and flowing. And the whole dock vibrating and humming with purpose ... the whole cannery shaking and belching and rattling out over the water ... all through the night ... this surreal motorized fantasy ... with little forklifts bouncing and scuttling around ... and lights glowing in the darkness and boats coming up to service and fuel the thing ... with their horns and their scurrying little creatures all on the deck ... and then the hold opening up ... disgorging its contents. Lines and cables and voices in the night ... screams and orders and pulleys and cranes ...

Yes, all of it ... the whole thing ... an amphibious attack on the senses. You quickly learn to block the unpleasant aspects out. You rearrange your brain, construct defense mechanisms. You filter everything out except that 20 percent you can run on.

6

▼

A WEEK HAS PASSED.

There is only work now. And the struggle to function.

I have been moved to the cannery line. A rattling drone of an operation with five million cans a minute bumbling down through the slender, metal-veined little tunnel. It was almost better than the cutting line at first. But it has its own death.

Supposedly, it's the easy line. You stand there ... with this loud, never-ending rattle and pop in your ears. All these cans ... hundreds ... thousands of them ... all sliding down their little canals where we stuff them with portioned fish taken from our little baskets nearby ... and every once in a while somebody comes over to replace the basket. And so you stand there stuffing fish into the cans as they come by, collecting in front of you in a widened portion of the canal, and you stuff them and wait for them to thin out ... and on they go ... marching and rattling by you. And every once in a while there is a clog up or a can has jammed going back into the main vein and they have to shut the machine down, and there is yelling and cursing as they try to get the operator's attention before the whole thing jams up. The first time this happened, about 150 cans ended up on the floor, and the supervisor comes over and questions the operator and it is an absurd mess taking nearly a half-hour to straighten out.

Sometimes when they can't get the damn thing to run correctly, the little fish boy (the local boy) runs over in his overalls and his boots. He brings his screwdrivers and his grease and proceeds to climb up there, tinkering and hollering and tapping and screwing and adjusting. Occasionally there is a little conference, and the supervisor and little Mr. Fix-It and some other moron stand there yapping and pointing and gesturing idiotically. Eventually, after some more yanking and turning, it coughs and sputters and starts up again.

One day I read the warnings and labels and copyrights all on the back of the machine. It turns out that this beauty was manufactured in 1929. Yes. Unbelievable! It's seen a World War. And a few others too. All those years. All those rattling hours. Yes. 1929. And they still repair this thing and make it work. It's unbelievable.

And so you stand there. Stuffing the cans as they go by. Stuffing a little bit of yourself in each time. And you smooth off the top and trim off any bones that may be sticking up.

The cans keep bouncing by. Off to other adventures. Off to crates and ovens and boxes and ships and trucks and out onto a supermarket shelf where they sit there smiling and obliging and polite.

7

▼

FRIDAY.

My life has become rain and mountains and fish and coffee and walking. I'm very high on marijuana at a place called Sandy Beach. I brought a small joint with me, and I'm enjoying the strange rhythm of my hand as it glides and twists across the page. My hand is very cold.

It is low tide. The rain of the last three days has just stopped. It is low tide and cold feet.

I am situated at the furthest end of the inlet, facing it lengthwise. It widens out toward the bay. I've been on the island fourteen days. Walking miles each morning and then later, after work, huddling in my small dome atop my wooden platform. I will not leave here without any money. I've decided that much.

Currently, I am trying to get a room in the dormitory at work with the young bearded Max. I requested it after a series of chance meetings with him at my morning indulgence of one hotcake at the cafe. He's the first. A pleasant sort. Rubs his beard. Complains about the food. Seems thoughtful. Quiet. Keeps to himself. Suitable rooming material.

8

▼

WEDNESDAY.

A day off today. Lying in my sleeping quilt … rain sweeping across the platform … wind blowing the tent almost over. I drifted in and out of sleep … lingering on a sort of threshold … asleep but not asleep. Getting up finally, walking the narrow path from my platform through the swamp to the cold bathroom. Washing my face, my neck. Thumbing a ride into town. Everything cold and wet and windy in the face, the day divided by an illegal steam shower at Island Fisheries. It's the other cannery here. Their showers are much nicer than the ones out at Ocean Queen, where I'm at.

Yes. I snuck into their bunkhouse late in the afternoon, pretended I worked there. I quickly put my toiletries and things down on a chair and stepped into a stall and pulled the curtain back. I turned on the water very hot and sat down on the floor of the tiny shower cross-legged away from the water and disappeared for a half-hour.

I finished and then dried off and put my clothes on and snuck back out. And then later back out in the streets of town again. Walking around, a bit hungry.

I stopped into the cafe for a cup of hot chocolate. A few captains and locals in there yapping it up. Talking this, that, and the other. Talking the season, talking their boat, talking the weather. I stayed there about three quarters of an hour, just sitting there in my chair and looking out the window. Soon I made it out and started walking back to my tent.

I can't think of anything but sleep. Ever. People who have gotten eight hours of sleep every night all their lives do not know the meaning of sleepiness. Working forty hours a week, they have no concept of it. No knowledge of ninety-six hours a week whatsoever. No knowledge of the hallucinations, the fantasies, the burning, heavy redness in the eyes.

And the mental states. There's a final extension that can only be described as the de-cloaking stage. When you look at someone when you're in the de-cloaking stage, it's not really their face or their body that you see anymore but more like an exposure and a caricaturing of all their innermost qualities. Qualities that sobriety always hides. It's like looking at them and seeing the painting that is them. As if the truth of them becomes so apparent that it reaches abstraction. They become a visual manifestation of their personality. Yes.

And everything else, too. It's simply being here. The assault on the senses makes everything run together. Like a strange film. A classroom experiment. Everything becomes green and white and analog. Strange faces. Strange bodies. Little boats floating upside down in the air. Aquatica and flotsam in the background. Scattered fossils and bits of foam drifting around here and there.

Or maybe I'm just coming unhinged.

9

▼

SUNDAY EVENING.

The cannery is a rainy, wet zoo. Obnoxious babbling workers shoving around, hollering.

It is cold and wet and steel choppers … everywhere. It is blood and water and fish heads. I stand there today, pulling eggs from the stomachs as the fish go by. The PVC pipe gets clogged. Some spillage over the edge. More hollering … more ugly dead faces turn around.

Your earplugs pop out. Over there a corner maybe … yes, a nice little dry place to take off your wet gloves and put your earplugs back in. Only the line, the machine, the clinking groaning bastard in front of you—it has you. It keeps you there. You cannot leave. You leave the earplugs out. It is very loud. You keep pulling eggs.

We are yanked from one position to another to keep everyone on his toes and in possession of job knowledge. We work the kinks out. One of the strangest jobs is "spray man." Yes. You stand beside a large revolving iron wheel, maybe seven or eight feet in diameter, with a set of twenty or thirty hooks that catch the fish off another part of the line and push them through a series of blades and brushes and scrapers to clean out the stomach cavity, and then to a final blade that cuts off the tails that collect down at the bottom of the drainage area. Yes. And this

drain will become clogged unless aided by a forceful stream of water
delivered from a high-pressure hose held by the "spray man."

Occasionally, a complete fish will plop down into the four or
five inches of water just beneath the blades, or else two or three will
enter the hook and blade wheel at the same time and lodge in there
sideways, preventing any other fish from traveling up, or simply wedge
themselves between the link and the frame. Whenever this happens
(and it happens frequently), I curse any and everything I can think of.
Basically, this means you have to reach up in there and pull the bastard
out without getting your rain gear caught in the machinery and your
arm cut open.

Yes. You pull your sleeves up and go turn your water down and
then walk back up to the machine and get down on your knees and
reach up in there ... your hand about six inches from the blades and
the hooks ... this deafening roar in your ears ... ice-cold water gently
misting in your face and eyes ... and you work the damn thing out very
carefully, preferably by the tail if available, and go carry it back up into
the trough for another try.

Performing this little chore only takes about half a minute or so,
but it starts to seem epic as the shift wears on ... when your legs and
your forearms and your hands and your back are already spent to the
point of collapse ... when you've done it ten or twelve times already
during the day.

Yes ... it'll be maybe ... ten in the evening ... fourteen hours
behind you ... two more to go. You'll be standing there in a daze ... the
machine droning on endlessly ... looking down at the drain with your
hose clamped down beside you ... directing the water out with your
hand. Sending the stream through a constant little program of locations
and maneuvers that you've developed to keep the tails and heads from
clogging up ... a little network of positions and angles of water ... two
seconds here ... ten seconds there ... a sweeping motion here ... a slow
arc there ... your forearms hot and thick and pulsating with fatigue ...
hollering and singing to keep awake ... singing any and every song you
can possibly think of in its entirety, loudly ... and some that you make
up for the occasion, and still no one can hear you.

You'll be standing there ... in your yellow rain slicker. Hood way
down over your eyes ... night has fallen ... artificial light flooding
the room ... the minutes passing on and on ... something out of a

hallucination or a dream. Thinking of your childhood. Thinking of sleep. Thinking of a large room in a castle with a roaring fire and a large chair and a young woman rubbing your shoulders.

And then you see it. Another fish has lodged up against the frame and will not hook. You stand there for a second looking at it in disbelief. You hate it. You hate this fish. It is idiotic, but you are tired. You are tired and you cannot believe you have to do this one more time.

And last night. Last night as I was preparing to complete this little task yet again, the wheel suddenly lets out a large groan and begins to clink violently and then stops altogether. Yes. The young dumb little bulldog with the serious face appears and climbs up in there with a little metal wrench in his hand. He's up inside the wheel. Looking around. Mr. Fix-It. He is a shit. (He's been here his whole life. Year after year. He behaves like an ass.) Yes. I would like to see him filleted and fed to whales.

He's tinkering, cursing, pushing, pulling. Yes. Much to my delight, a belt has slipped off somewhere. I stand there. Watching ... face dripping with water ... hose in my hand ... curled up and clamped down beside my torso with my elbow. Then suddenly I hear a crackling, death voice in my tired, offended ears.

It is Gorman, the Cro Magnon manager. I fantasized many times about seeing him filleted also. He should have been shoved off a dock as a teenager. I wished him up in the machine many times. He bellows out ... at 10:15 PM:

"Hey, don't just stand there with the fucking hose in your hand. I want this whole area cleaned up."

I ventured an attempt at explaining that usually another sprayer is on the other side as well. That I can't do it all by myself. Eventually give up.

And on it goes. Hour upon hour. My life in Petersburg is largely thus.

10

▼

Tuesday.

Many days have passed. Weeks. I have moved into a kind of dormitory for workers. A brown wooden halfway house at the south end of town. Am rooming with the young bearded Max. I have purchased a ticket out of here at the airport. The airport is a little aluminum building with a mile-long strip of asphalt just the other side of the city.

Yes. I didn't show up for work yesterday. I have had a pleasant weekend and now have a few weeks of shit to endure until my flight to Juneau in August.

11

▼

A DAY.

No mail. No nothing. A day spent in the bars in a desperate insane attempt to land a deckhand position. Possibly I would alter my departure and stay for the duration of the summer if this worked out. Anything seems preferable to the cannery. And the pay is higher. But there is nothing. Nothing but the shaking of heads. It looks as though I'll leave. I'm tired. And my resources are low. I'll have enough money to escape, though. I plan to head south. Way south. At least for a couple months or so. These last weeks and days here are like a prison sentence that I am trying to endure.

I walk the docks. I see big yachts. Shiny and clean and white, with mahogany trim and nice brass steering wheels. Old white-headed men, padding around ... taking it easy ... wiping and adjusting small little things absentmindedly. They're all retired. They all have money. They're all from someplace else. They're all just passing through. Slowly making their way up the coast. Stopping here and there. I would give anything to sail off with one of them. I'd go anywhere. Within the hour. Anywhere. Anywhere at all. South America. Hawaii. California. Some good food and drinks. Yes. I would smoke languidly on the deck. I would be in fine form. I would be in fine form and much of the time laughing. I'd serve the old goat and his wife in style. Sailing off once again. To wherever and whatever.

I even talked to a few of them today. I was desperate and down and delirious. I proceeded to offer my services as traveling companion, errand boy, and conversationalist to three or four boats. For as long as they needed me. They were so large. Mini white cruisers. Streamlined and graceful and sexy. I imagined the laughter of some curvy young thing filling the cabin—picked up especially for me.

Of course my offers were rejected kindly. I came crashing back down. Wandered off down the docks.

12

▼

FRIDAY.

A week has passed. Max has moved out. Couldn't take it anymore. Said he never wanted to see fish ever again. He is living on the black sailboat, *Anna Victoria*. He rented it for a month. It is haunted. The previous owner went insane three years ago trying to fix it up.

I sit here in bed munching a bubblegum lollipop. I'm still at the dormitory.

The beautiful coastline bores me. I only want to go to the library every day. I have no more questions. I only attempt to select circumstances and respond—or rather, they select me, and I try to intoxicate myself on whatever's there.

13

▼

WEDNESDAY.

Declined once more from presenting myself at work. Have spent the day smoking marijuana with some fat kid staying a few rooms down, as well as indulging in lengthy afternoon reading sessions of various accounts of Hitler, Caesar, Hannibal, etc., at the local library. Fascinating reads, and mysteriously, amid the uncertainty of my present circumstances, my spirits have lifted considerably. Afterwards a lovely nine-o'clock walk back to my room and the smoking of cigarettes.

However, upon entering my room, I found the belongings of another traveling worker conveniently placed in the corner of the bed opposite mine, and the bed made up and the sheets freshly changed.

I inspected his belongings. One Daniel Marra from Portland, Oregon. I am prepared for anything. Most likely an introduction and a small meeting will have to occur with him before I retire to bed.

I will return to work tomorrow. If I am released due to my unexplained absence, I will get drunk and celebrate. For my situation has seemed beyond description for quite some time now. Time passes as crude oil oozing from a small cold pipe. And I care nothing for the extra money and relative comfort that staying any longer would afford me in, say, Mexico, but am too preoccupied with trying to exist into the next day and in shortening the amount of work done before I leave, thus ensuring that my waning supply of patience and energy will not completely dry up, leaving me with the possibility of doing or saying something irrational and suicidal and sabotaging all my efforts.

14

▼

SUNDAY.

Am living on the *Anna Victoria* with Max. Have departed from work a few days ahead of schedule due to the fatigue and insanity experienced last night. Yes. At about the fifteenth hour, having just endured a ridiculous lecture from Gorman, I did him the favor ... and walked out.

I had been there six weeks. This morning, I turned in my rain gear, smoked a joint, and consumed a fine meal of omelets, bread, and coffee.

I have maybe $1,400 left after expenses. Splendid! The nightmare of cannery work is over. It seems already as if it never happened. All the endless hours. All the blood and fish and cold coughing wetness. The soaked sleeves. The stink and horror of fatigue. The assault on the senses. The absurdity and hopelessness and force of the situation. Sixteen hours a stretch. One day bleeding into the next.

But now, yes, yes ... no more! I have six days to loaf at the library and lounge on the boat. Most, most excellent.

15

▼

SATURDAY?

I am in a splendid mood and cannot think straight.

Last night Max and I had visitors from another cannery. Eight or ten people in all. Acquaintances mostly. And their acquaintances.

Yes. Everyone gathered around the table at the back of the boat. A couple of swaying little lanterns ... the creaking of wood. Everyone sitting around drinking beer ... asking if anyone had anything to smoke. I smile and creep up to the bow and procure a bag from my luggage and proceed to bring it back to the table and roll up a nice fat joint. Yes, perfect timing ... everyone suddenly happy and in good spirits ... ready for a small break from the gut-wrench of work.

Soon there is much laughter and revelry, culminating suddenly with a stool crumbling under Jesse, the fat kid from Ocean Queen.

Yes. Out of nowhere ... in the middle of a sentence, three hits into the joint, suddenly Jesse crashes to the floor like a meteor—from two or three feet up in the air, the legs of the stool lying cracked and broken beneath him. There is an instant of high, stunned silence, then all the boat explodes and convulses with laughter.

I tried to hold it back, but could not. And Jesse, taking it in stride and with style, lying on the floor ... chest heaving and shaking uncontrollably ... laughing harder than anyone ... ten or twenty seconds worth ... tears in his eyes ... completely loaded ... people gathered around trying to help him up ... finally between whoops and gasps he proclaims the boat booby-trapped. This sends everyone into another spasm of laughter. And him just lying there. A comedian. Refusing to get up. Still composed but ridiculously high, stunned and laughing. Trying to say something else. Something about a stool leg being up his ass.

All of us on the boat with tears in our eyes. A minute or two more, and Jesse slowly getting up, people behind him trying to help him ...

"Yeah, ya'll planned this shit out ... I know you did ... said watch this ... we gonna get high tonight ... gonna get hiiiighhh high ... and ya'll set me on this goddamn bar stool ... you knew it was a piece of shit ... goddamn ... somebody help get this stick outta my ass!!!"

I'm curled back against the wall with tears in my eyes, my stomach is hurting from laughing. It feels like I've ripped something in my gut. And Jesse, rambling on again. People are trying to hold him up at the shoulders.

"Damn that's some shit ... no, no I'm gonna stand up from now on, that's awright."

All of us trying to gain our composure. Jesse up on his feet now trying to put the bar stool back together. One leg is dangling off, one is on the floor, and the other is broken.

It's quiet for just a second, and then Max tells him not to worry about it and we all collapse into squeals and whooping again like little children. Jesse leaning now over the table, his big high face consumed with half talk, half gasping for air in between jerks of laughter.

"All ya'll muthafuckas ain't never gonna forget this when ya'll came to Alaska. I know ya'll ain't. Sorry-ass muthafuckas."

It goes on for ten more minutes ... dying down every so often, then the whole boat suddenly bursting and rollicking out over the docks again, each new wave brought on by the slightest snicker.

And then, a mere fifteen minutes later, Jesse sends us all to laughter yet again as he recalls someone in his apartment in Seattle calling 911 emergency services after thinking he was having a heart attack from some good smoke that Jesse had put him on.

"And I kept telling him, man, relax, you just high … that's just some good smoke, now sit back and relax 'cause you just high. And this muthafucka freakin' out 'n shit and callin' the fuckin' paramedics ta my house and shit and I said, 'Yo man, you call they ass up and tell them you awright' … but hell no, once you call that's it … they fuckin' comin'. You can't stop 'em. And they show up and shit and I'm hiding in the back closet and the whole fuckin' place smelling like weed and the paramedics are *in my house* … takin' a look at him and asking him had he been doing anything illegal recently … any illegal drugs, and I'm hearin' all this from the back closet, and they kept checkin' him out and tellin' him he's all right and I already knew he was all right. I tried ta tell his ass. And finally they leave and I went out and I was like, 'Yo, don't be fuckin' comin' over no more wantin' to get high 'n shit.'"

A night of nights. I had to take a walk down the dock later. Smoke cigarettes, remember it all, wipe tears from my eyes.

Alaska.

16

▼

MONDAY.

Nothing to do now but leave. I sit around on the deck, look at all the other rigs ... the fishing boats, the trawlers, the pleasure crafts, the yachts, the trollers, the skiffs. This whole place seems like a room that I'm about to turn around and walk back out of. It's funny, looking around ... knowing you won't be back.

I go see Ramone. A gifted, gone, sad case from Corvallis, Oregon. Tall, dark hair. Independent, composed. He's still at Swamp Shitty. He had the faith, until he came to Alaska. Every once in a while I would run into him on the street. It's not hard to do. We'd go off to the beach or the rainforest and get high.

I make my way out to his tent, scratch the side of it. It is fairly large. He's a pro. We sit down inside ... cross-legged, exchange greetings. Evidently he's been thinking.

"So you're leaving ... I will be too. Soon."

He looks off. I light a cigarette ... exhale.

"How are you?"

He looks up ... smiles, looks off again.

"You know ... I remember being back in Oregon ... I remember sitting around thinking ... yeah ... I'll hang out in Alaska for a while ...

It's got to be good in Alaska … everything unspoiled. But this cannery shit is for the birds."

He looks off.

"When I get back home, I'm going to cook my girlfriend this massive feast. And I can't wait to hit the beach. Shit. I can't wait to zip up my wetsuit and head down to the beach."

I'm sitting there looking at him. We worked on the line together for a while. We sprayed on each side of the wheel. He was the other "spray man." Every forty-five minutes or so, when it was time for him to clean some of the blood off the ceiling, he would knock me on the side of the leg with a stream of water from about fifteen feet off and I would look up at him and he would give a little nod of the head up toward the ceiling and I would back off and he would direct the water up at the little mess for a few seconds and then we would look back at each other with a little jerk of the head and drift back off into our own individual worlds until the next time.

Every once in a while, you remember somebody. For whatever reason, I'll remember Ramone. He had style … and a deep easy intelligence. No hang-ups … religious, political, social, or otherwise. And he was all there. And he recognized the Moment. Whatever it is. He recognized how absurd and ridiculous everything is. Us being in Alaska. Young. Looking for something. Anything. Sitting on the beach. Watching the eagles fight over salmon scraps. Watching the ships … the fishing boats … looking around at all the mountains and the white and the green … looking at the tiny cold little waves … at the rocks … at all the odd watery little things … the formations … the eddies and swirls and strings of plants … the scraps of wood … all the bits and pieces of everything washed up into our brains.

To live is to become. To become who you are. Sometimes you live more than others, and sometimes you live because you don't know what else to do. Through it all there is an odd thread, a strange continuity, and you try to remember something. There is an urge for some place, some point of reference.

In truth, we are held up by the frailest of notions. And even if these give way, it won't stop anything. The best you can do is try to get to the bottom of these notions and go from there. The only thing you'll find in life is life. And even then it doesn't matter. If you even try or not.

The choice is yours. You choose anyway. Maybe a life of addiction and separation. A calm life of work and money and commerce. An easy life of consuming and forgetting.

Each moment and each day ... is who you are ... and what you were.

I walk back to the boat.

Ramone, if you ever read these words, my friend ... know that in the midst of all the hell of those weeks and months ... through all the agony and the battles of mind and body ... through all the walks and the rainforests ... know that on our walks ... on our paths, the sun was always shining, man.

17

▼

TUESDAY.

Everything is moving very quickly. I have collected my luggage and my tickets and have journeyed to the airport in a taxi and am now preparing to board a small 707 that has landed somehow and pulled up to the building.

In a few minutes, I will be walking toward it. I am dumbfounded. It appears as though it will actually take off with me on it and fly out of here.

I don't know what to say. It is enough that I am leaving.

18

▼

AUGUST. SEATTLE
INTERNATIONAL AIRPORT.

I have escaped from Petersburg.

Am waiting on a midnight flight to Austin rerouted through Houston. As compensation, I was given a $300 America West Airline voucher good for travel in Mexico. Yes! Most, most excellent.

It is hard to put a name to the feeling. Mostly relief, but something else as well. A certain emptiness. And a sad, dazed comfort ... a sort of absence of feeling.

And now elevator music is flowing gently down through the terminals. I'm sitting in a large seating area at an unused gate facing the window. Passengers amble by in the reflection. The airport is largely empty. The night planes take off and land inside their little blue rows of neon. Little tractors are scurrying around their masters. Everything so modern and urban and symphonic. Everything so *Blade Runner*. Here comes the music again. Everything is designed for you ... for human comfort. Airports are different at night. There is a special urban glow. The volume is turned down. Everything so inoffensive. So ordered. So polite.

PART 4

▼

I

▼

SEPTEMBER. SAN MIGUEL, GUANAJUATO, MEXICO.

I am at the Hotel Vianey. Off Mesones near the plaza. Yes. I've made it somewhere at last now again. San Miguel de Allende. Twelve hundred dollars in my shirt pocket. Traveler's checks. I've got a couple of months to play with now. I'm sitting at a table with a small portable typewriter at the second-floor window of my hotel. It's about 10:00 PM. The window is open and I am chain-smoking.

I look out at the night and the winding stairs and the rooftops and the lights scattered here and there on the mild easy mountains. There is the faint sound of music filtering through from the plaza and the restaurants and the flow and chatter of Spanish-speaking voices. A woman walks by talking to her husband. Her high heels click and clatter on the streets and disappear.

It's funny. I sit here. Looking out the window. Plane rides, airports, taxis, customs, taxis again, a four-hour bus ride from Mexico City, and then another taxi to the plaza where I get out to go try to find a hotel.

Once you're in a room, everything's all right. But when you first get out of the taxi and it's dark, you're not too sure for a second. I didn't know really where I was except somewhere downtown. I walked off with my luggage on my back and looked for hotel signs.

Three tries later and I'm in. My broken Spanish pulled through. And then there you are. You've made it someplace else. From an island off the Alaskan coast to an airport in Seattle, through Houston and Austin for a while and now to a hotel room just off a main street in a little hill town north of Mexico City.

It's been here four hundred years. Left over from the silver boom, the Spaniards.

Eventually I decide to step out for a little walk. I wander around. There is very nice European colonial-style architecture everywhere. Stone-patterned streets. Very appealing. Very soft. Little groups of people collecting here and there. In cafes. On street corners, on benches and steps. Strolling around. Socializing. Laughing. Little stone cathedrals, bells, side streets. Large wooden doors with heavy black handles. I decide to head down to the plaza. Yes. I walk past the neatly trimmed little bushes and the benches and walkways and fountains. With the families and young lovers and old men and the occasional little dog running around sniffing and exploring. Little scooters and taxis lined up off to the side. A little flame flickering in a taco stand. Cigarette vendors. Magazine vendors. Music.

I wander around for a while, eventually head back to my hotel. I sit down again, laugh, look off at the wall, light another cigarette.

2

▼

TUESDAY.

The faces I've looked at seem kind. I don't care about seeing any sights. I just want to sit here in this room and walk on these cobblestone streets. These sexy, winding, cobblestone little streets. And who cares how I got here. I can't even remember how I heard about it.

3

▼

WEDNESDAY.

The day has passed like a love scene. It is over now, and time has resumed. And yes, one of the more interesting little pieces from my symphony today began as I sat in the loveliest, most sensual, most mood-altering place I could find: the Cathedral Parroquia de San Miguel. Yes. A little feast for the eyes. They put some work into this. I almost wanted to be Catholic.

Yes. It was lovely. Bathed in beauty. I was about twenty pews back. In the right arm of the cross layout.

All the statues, religious figures ... somber, pretty Mary smiling gently down on the offering box, more mannequins, sculptures, cherubs, archangels, saints, five or ten more Virgins, three or four Mary Magdalenes, and a profuse flowering of Christs done up in glass, laying down, trimmed in gold, up on a wall, flanked by angels, painted on the ceiling, and of course, one in the center, over the priest's chair, nailed on the cross, head handsomely down, looking majestic, wronged, noble, peaceful, and perfect.

And everywhere gold and chandeliers and ornate trimming and satin and red velvet and polished oak and smooth curvy stone and twinkling bits of glass and candlesticks and marble.

I sat there, and presently a few more sinners began to file in. But alas, I was so intoxicated that I didn't think of leaving until it was too late. Yes. The lights came slowly on. The large door swung shut and suddenly, time for Mass! Oh no. This wouldn't do. But it had to. And did. I couldn't leave then. Go walking back down the aisle to wrestle with the creaky, iron, noisy door. Besides, the singing had begun. I immediately started rummaging through my head trying to remember what their little ceremony was ... about the wafer and the drops or something. Surely it wasn't required duty for everyone. This wouldn't do at all. Potential for disaster, fiasco, and *faux pas* all in one. Yes.

But luckily, the whole affair was none too charismatic. Though a couple of times the sign of the cross caught me off guard. (I did it myself as well.) And the kneeling down for prayers or saints or something. I was always a few seconds behind everyone else. But soon I began to relax. I thought of the Mayans, the Egyptians, the Greeks. All the mystery religions. All the concepts. All the temples. All the moments like this all through time all over the earth. All the wine. All the ecstasy.

On it went. A few more prayers. A few more songs. A small sermon followed by more prayers. It was turning out somewhat pleasant, though I quickly grew tired of all the standing and kneeling.

After what seemed about an hour the service was dismissed. I remained seated with my head down to discourage any conversations in Spanish. Finally the whole crew cleared out, and I felt it safe enough to venture outside.

I walked outside, ambled around for a while before deciding on Posada de San Francisco for a drink.

"Si, señor. Como esta?"

I sat down. Ordered a beer.

4

▼

A DAY.

Mmm. Mexico. I feel myself coming alive again. I wake up, keep laying there for half an hour, eventually put on some clothes. Walk out. Down toward the plaza. The day begins to move through me. New and slow and warm. Like a mild sunny greeting. The hours preparing to pass. Out in front of me are little faces with dark hair. Old women in scarves bobbing and moving around. Ambling here and there. Crossing the street. Standing on the corner. Men loading a truck. Little workers repairing some stone. I keep walking. Down, down, down and then turning a corner on Calle Hidalgo and stepping onto a narrow stone sidewalk now. All alongside me are little houses and black iron and balconies and staircases winding up and down. I look up. The street stretches out before me. Further down toward the plaza, the crowd is beginning to thicken slightly.

I walk on. Glancing about. A man is spraying a hose, standing inside an open doorway. A small dog is sniffing around on the ground and pausing every once in a while to look up before running off and disappearing. The occasional car is plodding along over the cobblestone. There is a man pushing a cart and then a well-dressed couple. I amble along, the buildings rising up on each side of me.

And then later on at Posada Carmina. Drinking Dos Equis in the courtyard. There is a canopy over my table.

I'm feeding the birds and overhearing a conversation a couple of tables over. Americans. Retired. From Corpus Christie.

"Honey, we still haven't got A&E. If it weren't for NBC, I wouldn't have had anything to look at last night on television."

The old man nods. He's reading a newspaper, smoking Benson & Hedges ... 100s.

She turns around to her sister.

"You shoulda seen it, Nora. It was so interesting. By the way ... "

"And honey, order me some more coffee, would you?"

She continues on.

I keep feeding the birds. There's about a hundred up in the tree. A pleasant cascade of chirping and peeping. I call the waiter over to ask how you say "bird" in Spanish.

"*Como se dice, en Español?*" I point at them.

"Ah ... "

He pronounces the word slowly. We repeat it to each other, making sure I've got it right.

He walks off. I look down again at the birds, keep repeating it. I try different versions. Keep dropping bread.

5

▼

A DAY.

Mmm. I have found the library. *La Biblioteca Publica*. About twenty thousand English titles. More than enough for a brief stay! Yes. And there is something else in the library that has caught my eye. She teaches English to a little group of young mice. She seems young. Not more than eighteen. I can't tell whether she is Mexican or Italian. It does not matter. Every afternoon now I come sauntering past on my way to English fiction and there she is, leaning over a small table in the shade.

" ... okay after me ... one ... juannnn ... two ... tuuuuuu ... three ... threeeeee."

She might be perfectly worthless, but I am somewhat fascinated and aroused at the sight of her teaching English to these tiny little creatures.

Yes. Each day now I arise and lunch at about two at Posada de San Francisco. I order *enchiladas suizas, negra modela, cafe con leche, ciggaros delicadas*. There is a perfect view of the plaza. I sit there, eat, drink, stare contentedly. Smoke. Order more coffee. At about three-thirty, I ask for the bill, exit, and turn the corner up Calle Hidalgo toward the library.

At about seven, the library closes and I walk down to Parque Benito Juarez and stroll through the lanes, smoking cigarettes and deciding where I should go … for dinner!

6

▼

SATURDAY.

Drunk now again! Finally. I couldn't resist the liquor store on the way home from dinner tonight. Twenty-one pesos and a fine bottle of red.

Opening the damn thing up, I had to push the cork through. It wouldn't rise properly. But this didn't stop me. I drained the bits and crumblings and poured myself a lovely delicious red glassful. It all comes back. The red strong taste in the mouth, the excess formation of saliva. Ah yes. The heaviness in the head, the short-term memory loss, the smell, the silly confident sensation …

I stagger around, walk to a corner, glance lazily around the room. My eyes fall on my little stash of money on the nightstand. It's running low these days. Already. And I only recently escaped from Alaska. Everything's always running out. Money. Time. Fuel. I wouldn't care if it all went to hell now at this point.

Yes. I'm imagining a giant invisible star. Four atoms hydrogen, one atom helium. Locked in embrace. Having nowhere to go, nothing to be. Suspended in inky black pre-nothing.

"Therefore, we, the heavy elements, by decree of all that is relative, transitory, and completely and momentarily beautiful, hereby ordain and declare these works of genius to be self-evident … that all molecules rest differently … and that all pursue ridiculous paths of physics, beauty, and the pointlessness of evolution … "

(Hack, coughing … commotion.)

I try to give a speech, fall down, pass out.

7
▼

WEDNESDAY.

It rains every afternoon now for about an hour. The last two days it has caught me. And not just a rain. A downpour. A forty-five-minute monsoon. The streets turn to rivers. There is general commotion and the mad rush for taxis, rides, and shelter.

Today I was down near the plaza when it hit. I walked calmly across the street to an arch over a hotel. Shoes soaked. Cigarettes ruined. There I stood for about twenty minutes and waited until the cows that were stampeding and fighting over taxis thinned out just a bit. It kept coming down. Hard. A Popsicle stick floated by. A taco stand was pushed away to cover.

I am standing there looking at it all when suddenly it hits me. It hits me that I am alive. Alive! Meaning … it doesn't matter! It's not cold. Who cares!

And so I began walking back to my hotel down the center of a little cobblestone street in the rain. Yes. I walked on. Water dripping off the chin. My clothing soaked. My hair streaming down the side of my face.

Plip plop. Plip plop. On through the rain. My arms and legs and breathing all synchronized. Plip plop. Walking and breathing. Walking and breathing. Strange how I never liked it before. Oh, but I like it now!

8

▼

Monday night.

It always happens when you least expect it.

I met Nina on Friday. Four days ago. I was just off the plaza during the Independence Day festivities. Her and her girlfriend were sitting on the curb opposite me, looking young and lovely. The moment was there and not to be thrown away. I ventured across the street and sat down beside them. It turns out they speak English.

The next two days proceeded to float by in a strange, pleasant haze. I let myself go completely.

Nina was young. Nineteen. But highly intelligent, sensitive, and affectionate. She kept asking me question after question in this lovely little accent, all the while flashing her lashes and staring deeply into my eyes. We talked for twenty or thirty minutes. She was from Guadalajara. Up for the weekend. Eventually we parted, but not before agreeing to meet the next day at Posada Carmina.

Yes. The next day at noon I come walking in, and there she is. Sitting at a perfect little table with a canopy over it in the back corner of the patio right out of some afternoon dream. I stroll toward her. We kiss lightly on the cheek and sit down to lunch. Soon we are smiling at each other over the menus and chatting and asking the other what they are going to order.

I put down my menu.

"Have you ever traveled outside of Mexico?"

"Oh yes. I went to … to … Los Angeles. It was nice. But very … expensive."

"Did you like it?"

"Yes."

I smile. The waiter walks up to take our order.

Soon our coffees arrive. He walks back off. We keep glancing up to look at each other. A bird lands on the patio.

"I'm glad you made it, Nina."

She starts laughing.

"Me too."

She looks down.

"Do you like Mexico, Gerald?"

"I do, actually."

After lunch I suggest a stroll to the park. I forgot who I was. Didn't care. We walk down through the narrow cobblestone streets past the balconies and the restaurants and make our way down to the south end of the city and into Parque Benito Juarez. We explore the little lanes and walkways of the park. Eventually we find a bench. The moment came, and we begin to kiss.

Later we are staring at one of the fountains, and I am supplying dialogue for the birds as they come up to the edge of the water. Yes. And these birds were feeling rather testy and irritable. They questioned why they were coming for a drink since they weren't very thirsty to begin with.

I go on and on. I time their departures perfectly and build up to it each time with the sudden recollection of an appointment to which one of them is about to be late. This little game goes on for five or ten minutes. It is very pleasant, and she is laughing. She is laughing, and I am suddenly aware of the day passing and consciously endeavor to forget this and sink deeper and deeper into it.

We walk back through the streets. Slowly. Lazily. All the way back up to the plaza. We sit looking at little children, at more fountains.

Smiling. Glancing at each other. I fall out of time. I think of us. Old. Gone. The city still there. With new lovers. New days.

Suddenly she puts her lips in my ear.

"I would like to go to your room with you."

When it's there, it's there, and all you have to do is drift with the moment.

We get up and begin walking back up to my hotel. Sometimes a day is a creation unto itself. It has a beginning and end. It has flow and curve and beauty. And it brings itself to you.

We turn in from the street underneath a little sign and walk across a large patio and to a corner and up a flight stairs. I lead her down a hall overlooking a small garden and turn left to a door. I unlock it. She walks in, and I close it behind her and pull the shutters together. We walk over to the bed and I sit her down and ease her head back onto the pillows. Her hair is straight and silky thick. It begins to rain outside.

Later on we are smoking cigarettes in bed. Listening to it rain. Slightly amazed.

Two days is never enough. But it's all you ever get. Two days here and there in a flood of decades. It's almost Monday now, and Nina is back in Guadalajara. Personally, I expect the years to pass quickly for me from here on out. Twenty-six and then forty and more.

The last night at dinner it all came pouring out of me. She had asked a very simple innocent question like what was I going to do back in Austin or what I liked and didn't like in life or some such. A few seconds passed and then ... *"uh-oh ... man the harpoons ..."*

At first there is a cracking and bending of wood and rigging. A jarring boom and the overlaying of masts and lines followed by a loud extended creaking as the front third of the ship gives way and separates slightly. And then you can see it. A bulging snout, magnificent and glistening. Eight or ten feet across. The head wedged in but seeming calm and without further struggle. Here and there small shreds of cartilage and blubber exposed to the air and a few rivers of burgundy sap beginning to flow. And through water and confusion a few feet down, a lone solitary eye, bathed in silver. A single black orb.

She takes my hand. At once I feel a bit odd. Slightly uneasy. I hadn't wanted to lead her this quickly onto deck. Especially since we both were about to leave, it seeming pointless and superfluous.

"Do you have to go back to work, Gerald? You can come live in Guadalajara. Maybe you can teach English."

"Think about it Gerald. Could you? It would be ... how do you say it ... perfect. I could ... I could take care of you. No?"

There is a long pause. Maybe a minute or so.

"Nina ... "

"No. Sshhh. I know. Listen ... I had a wonderful time with you."

There is nothing more to do. We pay and leave, embrace outside. By now it's 10:30 PM and her bus leaves for Guadalajara at eleven.

Walking down the sidewalk now to a fleet of taxis. Not knowing what to say. It could be anywhere. Down any street in any city in any decade of any century in any country in the civilized world. And the rest of it, too. It is the moment of departure. It always comes. It'll come again and again. Life is one big good-bye. You wave your hand for fifty years.

You feel anxious and terribly sad and maybe even a bit sick. There is a deep staring into the eyes and an attempt to fix an image in your mind of the moment. Promises are made. We kiss again and again. Embrace.

Then she is inside the taxi. We stare at one another. The car lingers a bit longer. It begins to pull away. I stand there waving. She is looking back at me and waving through the glass. The car turns, disappears down a side street.

I stand there for a long time looking down the street after her. I walk down to the plaza and sit down in the dark.

9

▼

MONDAY.

Maybe I should have gone with Nina. All this has sent me to thinking. Something. Something like I can't do it again. Find it all and bring it together one more time. The process. The days and weeks of waiting and scrounging around. And then finally some repetitive grind of a job. Your things moved into another room. A new place and you are working again and it is shocking and hateful. The gate closes shut on you once again and you have begun a new page and you are lost in another set of workweeks. Tiring and tiresome and stretching into months.

IO

▼

FRIDAY.

My last week has ended. I leave and don't say a thing. I lounge on the roof and fireworks paint the sky. It is another celebration here. Such is the present state of affairs. I anticipate nothing. Have become nothing.

I am thinking of how I am about to go eat breakfast. I am going to have boiled eggs, toast, strawberries, and coffee.

I have nowhere to go. Everything is stretched out before me. I only have to pick a road and go meandering down once more onto the plains. Or rather, lose my balance and trip and fall down whatever path is nearby. Either way it's the same. Here it is and here we go.

PART 5

I

▼

November. Austin, Texas.

Aaron is meditating. He's off in the nether regions. I've been here two weeks now. My back hurts and I wish I had a drink.

We've just returned from dinner. Thai Surprise. Phat Thai.

It seems everybody's going somewhere in life. That's the first thing I've noticed. Everybody's got plans.

Aaron's a perfusionist now. A link in the hospital chain. He has to be on standby all hours of the day and night in case one of the old tickers goes out and they need to do some mending. Just today he had two open-heart surgeries and one other minor.

He's back there now in his room. I am being quiet while he meditates. He's dreaming of the higher planes. Dreaming the lotus and floating on a halo. Dreaming three feet in the air and carried by a chant. He's drifting through toyland. He loves it. He can take a shit without having to wipe. He flushes with a thought and then it's on to the Emerald City.

*　　　*　　　*　　　*

And so, you find yourself back in civilization ... dazed and reaching for your sunglasses. Everything is supercharged and ultra-normal, with electronic urban hustle. Everywhere this disjointed little parade crawling around and multiplying and becoming and processing. Out in the streets and all in the buildings. All this information and television and computing. All this relay and transferal of images and devices and concepts and amounts. This nonstop circus going on every day all over the world. Everywhere you go, this overload of business and money and five-headed hydras. This gluttonous, greedy stampede for happiness.

Nobody knows and everybody knows ... and it's all there ... like vibrating energy, like electrons. Irritated. Nowhere to go, except in a circle. And no reason either. And who cares about the reason. As long as it's processing. As long as it's changing. Into something! Anything! Everything!

Yes. But it takes huge numbers of people to do this. Huge numbers of people to supply enough alternative passageways so that the money and energy sources can be revved up enough to produce the motion. So what do you have? There's a name for it. A name for what has happened. A name for our age. We are ... yes ... The Age of Mediocrity! Mediocrity has triumphed! Mediocrity is victorious! Mediocrity is the Ideal! Mediocrity is excellence!

2

▼

FRIDAY.

It's hard to believe I am back. Everything's a blur. Aaron is in Dallas. Visiting his sister. He has been good enough to take me in until I get my own place again. Aaron is a saint.

It's Saturday night. I look at walls. I'm getting sleepy. But wait. I don't want to go to bed. I want to just *sit* on this bed and look at pictures. Pictures in magazines maybe.

I sit around. Mostly stunned. I seem afflicted. I don't believe in anything. And I have no ambition. I just want to hop on a carousel ... a long oval carousel. I just want to go around and around and around. I will find one. Yes. And it's going to be oh so slow. So very, very slow. Slower than living. Slower than walking. Slower than all the planets everywhere.

Mmm. But on to the subject of the commode. Yes. It has a slow leak. Like so many other things in life. You constantly have to turn it off and refill it after each use, or just leave it on and listen to the damn thing struggle to refill every fifteen minutes or so. Yes. It's such an interesting little subject for me. The concept I'm speaking of ... of something not working. The proverbial "It's broken." A little object or machine or mechanism, or any type of instrumentation, measurement system, or device not doing what it was designed and meant to do, for whatever idiotic and ridiculous reason. It's so strange ... so indicative of something. That things always eventually break. That that's the natural state of rest or being. The realization of change and decay and locked disorder.

But every morning Aaron comes to check on me, bless him. To make sure I haven't rolled off the bed the wrong way. To make sure I haven't twisted my noggin or damaged my chakras. He's my savior.

He says I am preparing myself for my next life, in which I will find Enlightenment.

In Wot mons! Wot longs and leens!

3
▼

WEDNESDAY.

I've found a job. Irrational Business Machines, Incorporated! I come home at midnight and just sit. Sit and smoke on the porch ... bored with my planet. Light years have passed. I've traversed the galaxy, but still one runs out of money. Sooner or later one always runs out of money.

And I am waiting on a computing device from Bern. Yes. He could make himself useful. I haven't spoken to him in several months. We dropped out of college together. He said if I ever needed anything to call him. I did!

But he's holding out on me. Says he's got to wait until the first of next month. He's lying. He thinks this is funny. Me needing a computing device. He has no idea what I need to do.

Now he's in Aspen or Boulder or something ... eating steak. And running his business. Him and Morton. (They keep trying to get me to come up there and work for them.) Oh, and fucking his spoiled princess, Regina. Yes. Regina with her seven-thousand-dollar breasts. Regina. Symbol of success. Symbol of credit cards and takeovers. The trophy wife. Symbol of bank mergers, Donna Karan. I'm picturing them walking into a party at The Omni. A reception. A convention of fartmasters and business thinkers and tech money. Regina. Yes. Suddenly, Regina entering. There she is. Sculpted and magnificent ... and those breasts. Yes. All the eyes ... all the lights flooding down on her. The drum roll. The mild applause. Bern grinning like an idiot ... he's dressed in a tux. Six feet tall.

A bit of conversation at the other tables as they walk over for drinks ...

"Yes, well, he's obviously doing well for himself ... yes, she does look stunning ... I bet she's a bitch."

Yes, all this and more. And, I confess ... I lust after her myself. One can't help it. And she can talk even—that is, when she's not throwing a tantrum. I'm getting aroused just thinking of her.

Once we were drunk at a hotel. In the lobby. She started mouthing off about painting. The Impressionists, the Realists. Spouting off names. She was sitting there inebriated, uninhibited, dressed in a short tight little business suit. Bern was somewhere else upstairs, banging on a piano, delighted with himself.

It's hard not to look at her. We continued to talk, get drunk. More art, more cigarettes. More Pissarro, Van Gogh. More Cezanne, more wine, more cigarettes, more Courbet.

My head began to get heavy, and after a while Bern returned and we decided that a cabaret was in order. So then it was off to Sugars, where they both insisted upon buying me table dances. Yes. They found this quite humorous. Watching my expressions while young girls squirmed and gyrated in front of me. I went with it. I didn't care. I was feeling buzzed and empty and titillated.

They giggle at my trollishness. They like my unrehearsed energy, my untrained responses. They get a certain pleasure from seeing me teased.

And then at last, we had our fill. All three of us. Bern reached into his deep pockets and paid for the drinks. We walked out to his four-door sedan, drove off. Swerving, running stop signs.

They dropped me off at my room.

4

▼

FRIDAY.

In the middle of the night, you can sit drunk and stupid and timeless and huge and feel completely free to paint masterpieces or machine-gun your neighbors or narrate the continuing crisis while fleeing the jaws of your job and your piss-ant circumstances.

Mmm. I fancy being alone in the house like this. Aaron is in Beaumont or some such ridiculousness. I stand in halls … drink alcoholic beverages … lurk in closets … take long baths.

Tonight I have found some painkillers and am preparing to disappear down a long, lovely labyrinth of narcotic drowsiness. It's the only logical thing to do at present. Even now, I am getting excited at the long sleep I will drift off to in an hour or so. I am always so welcome in the arms of intoxication …

5

X.

I drink and am drunk. Tonight it is a lonely gesture at fertility. I salute Pan. I am envious. I am Pan.

I am shy and cruel to the Asian girls at work, but I really would like to have any or all of them. I sit there each day idly performing my little duties ... off on a seven- or eight-minute fantasy ... in a hut ... the eighth Shang Dynasty ... a hut in a lagoon ... with tight dark little eyes and choppy little round young laughs.

It is common, yes. But I can't help it. I run with it. The hours pass. I sit there and the evening fades. I am bored and desperate. My youth passing in front of my eyes ... late in the evening ... second shift ... artificial light ... a computing factory ... my latest travels behind me ... noises ... machines ... whirring ... a small alarm ... parts snapping into place ... a blip here and there ... an announcement ... a ready prompt.

Yes. Sitting there thinking any and everything. How to continue. How to escape.

The hours continue to pass, and with them little bits of you.

6

X.

I have to struggle along with little debts to the City of Austin Traffic Court. New licenses, overdue fees for my sportster, etc. It seems I didn't leave my affairs in order when I decided to take off to Alaska. Naturally.

I am working the present angle now from inside a prison. A prison of circumstance and money. It catches you again and again. I claw and connive and wait for it to pass.

It's all perfect and absurd. I am taken aback by the smallness and the obviousness of it. These little things that can kill you. All these rules and regulations and payments. These tiny little monsters. Bearing their weapons into your back.

And you attempt to thump them off, one by one. And they are replaced time and time again. And you continue to flick them off. Cursing and laughing and trying not to disappear beneath the petty huge weight of their mindless gathering.

And meanwhile, I am working away the days. In the manufacturing facility. Surrounded by lull and defeat. By normalcy and obscenity and compromise.

I only want to hold on to this one little frame of time tonight. To crawl up inside and laugh and sleep and disappear. I have it here right now with me. I caress it. I stretch it out.

And for a little while yet there is the music. I will sleep soon and awaken to the factory. To symmetry and metal and microchip. To lines and faces and eight new hours.

X.

I think ahead to senseless decades. To loneliness and supernovas. To music and misfires.

I am in a new room now. East 31st and Speedway. My own apartment again. My days line up on limbs outside the window. Young and old and everything in between. Something physical and ethereal ... winged for dumb flight.

I would like to visit the Asian girls, it is true. And I will. I have one in mind.

Yes. But I feel stranded. I stand on tall cliffs ... wind blowing ... scowling ... scanning the horizon for life-forms. I like to see who visits my floating forest ... who sees my floating fits.

I have no faith or love, just a natural attachment, enhanced by the senses. I sit here ... in pre-galactic center. I want to continue on with sex and magic. With physics and form. With sun-sex and fusion. With chromosome and curve and micro-lust.

The future. It's always in an orgasm. Star birth and stellar dust and gravity and then heat and cold and planets and then more heat and cold and then soil and roses and humans computing ...

8

▼

X.

Planet Earth. Human English. Average sun. Nondescript common spiral galaxy. Insignificant cluster in the L7 sector. Yes, and it might as well be anything at all, at any time ... according to any Einstein.

Tonight it is a black dog ... barking his nights up our tired backs, and they fall from us and we shake them off. We shake them off and get ready for more.

9

▼

December 31st.

I am drunk and high and pawing at the air. I laugh, drool, look off in monkey wonder.

It seems so silly, the passing of another year. The horns blare. The drinks pour.

Later the trees are already bored again. The wind is preoccupied. Everything is stuck in molasses once more. Even the galaxies. Wandering and fertile and tiny. Everything just there somehow. Microscopic and huge and deaf. Everything irritated and volatile and female. Bursting with cancer and beauty, but hung there all the same. Nailed to its source. Like an electron or a dog or a planet.

What I would not say tonight. To anyone. Remember, it is now as it is with you. Something there. Always and never.

The time has come for all the bent, the dazed, the gesturing fallen few. The time has come for more precious nothing. Extended years of days … tumbling down onto one another. Falling down a giant funnel of Time. It is cruel even to itself.

I would speak of poems and days off. Of factories and arrests and months traveled. Of money and of none. Of frequent lingering stillnesses and the return to intimacies.

There is a slow creeping smile in life. Even in death. I smirk, salute the flow. The carbon, spewing micro flow … sailing down itself. Through centuries and worlds and seconds. Bursting with pain. With singularity and sex. With beauty and concept and simple staccato.

And on and on we all go. Down the streets. Down all our streets. Trying loose change in odd machines. Gamblers we are. Laying it down. Always ready for the last one. Every one a last one. Fixated on a thing that moves. Upon motion and circumstance. Working some spare color into a makeshift mix.

We try another brush maybe. Another palette. We tell her to sit still.

Blue #2.

Yellow #4.

We dabble in it.

Terry Midkiff was born in Houston in 1970. He grew up in North Carolina and Texas. His work has appeared in *Mobius, the Poetry Magazine.*

Printed in the United States
By Bookmasters